WHEN THE EARL WAS WICKED

Forever Yours Series

STACY REID

WHEN THE EARL WAS WICKED is a work of fiction. While reference might be made to actual historical events or existing locations, the names, characters, places, and incidents are either the product of the author's imagination or are used fictitiously, and any resemblance to actual persons, living or dead, business establishments, events, or locales are entirely coincidental.

All rights reserved. No part of this book may be reproduced in any form by any electronic or mechanical means—except in the case of brief quotations embodied in critical articles or reviews —without written permission.

First Edition March 2019

Edited by AuthorsDesigns
Copy edited by Gina Fiserova
Proofread by Monique Daoust
Cover design and Formatting by AuthorsDesigns
Stock art from Period Images

Copyright © 2019 by Stacy Reid

Dusean, always and forever.

FREE OFFER
SIGN UP TO MY NEWSLETTER TO CLAIM YOUR FREE BOOK!

To claim your FREE copy of Wicked Deeds on a Winter Night, a delightful and sensual romp to indulge in your reading addiction, please click here.

Once you've signed up, you'll be among the first to hear about my new releases, read excerpts you won't find anywhere else, and patriciate in subscriber's only giveaways and contest. I send out on dits once a month and on super special occasion I might send twice, and please know you can unsubscribe whenever we no longer zing.

Happy reading!
Stacy Reid

PRAISE FOR NOVELS OF
STACY REID

"**Duchess by Day, Mistress by Night** is a sensual romance with explosive chemistry between this hero and heroine!"—*Fresh Fiction Review*

"From the first page, Stacy Reid will captivate you! Smart, sensual, and stunning, you will not want to miss **Duchess by Day, Mistress by Night**!"—*USA Today bestselling author Christi Caldwell*

"I would recommend **The Duke's Shotgun Wedding** to anyone who enjoys passionate, fast-paced historical romance."—*Night Owl Reviews*

"**Accidentally Compromising the Duke**—Ms. Reid's story of loss, love, laughter and healing is all that I look for when reading romance and deserving of a 5-star review."—*Isha C., Hopeless Romantic*

"**Wicked in His Arms**—Once again Stacy Reid has left me spellbound by her beautifully spun story of romance between two wildly different people."—*Meghan L., LadywithaQuill.com*

"**Wicked in His Arms**—I truly adored this story and while it's very hard to quantify, this book has the hallmarks of the great historical romance novels I have read!"—*KiltsandSwords.com*

"One for the ladies...**Sins of a Duke** is nothing short of a romance lover's blessing!"—*WTF Are You Reading*

"**THE ROYAL CONQUEST** is raw, gritty and powerful, and yet, quite unexpectedly, it is also charming and endearing."—*The Romance Reviews*

OTHER BOOKS BY STACY

Series Boxsets

Forever Yours Series Bundle (Book 1-3)

Forever Yours Series Bundle (Book 4-6)

Forever Yours Series Bundle (Book 7-9)

The Amagarians: Book 1-3

Sinful Wallflowers series

My Darling Duke

Her Wicked Marquess

Forever Yours series

The Marquess and I

The Duke and I

The Viscount and I

Misadventures with the Duke

When the Earl was Wicked

A Prince of my Own

Sophia and the Duke

The Sins of Viscount Worsley

An Unconventional Affair

Mischief and Mistletoe

A Rogue in the Making

The Kincaids

Taming Elijah

Tempting Bethany

Lawless: Noah Kincaid

Rebellious Desires series

Duchess by Day, Mistress by Night

The Earl in my Bed

Wedded by Scandal Series

Accidentally Compromising the Duke

Wicked in His Arms

How to Marry a Marquess

When the Earl Met His Match

Scandalous House of Calydon Series

The Duke's Shotgun Wedding

The Irresistible Miss Peppiwell

Sins of a Duke

The Royal Conquest

The Amagarians

Eternal Darkness

Eternal Flames

Eternal Damnation

Eternal Phoenyx

Single Titles

Letters to Emily

Wicked Deeds on a Winter Night

The Scandalous Diary of Lily Layton

CHAPTER 1

London, 1840

Shortly before eight o'clock on a Wednesday evening, Lady Verity Elizabeth Ayles knocked on a particular door at 86 Eaton Square, Eaton Square Gardens. To any passing onlooker, she presented as a fashionably attired woman with an elaborate hat covering her vibrant auburn hair and a dark veil obscuring her face. A black umbrella was clutched in one of her hands, and the other hand once again lifted the lion head knocker and slammed it insistently against the large oak door.

All delicate inquiry had said the man she wanted to see would be at home tonight. Despite the preeminence of his title and family's history, he was not welcomed in most drawing rooms, ballrooms, and gentlemen's clubs. Or so the rumors whispered.

The door was wrenched open, and a quite large man filled the doorway. It took all of the fortitude she'd gained over the years to not wilt from his imposing frame. She drew a deep breath, trying to calm the wild pounding of her heart. She cleared her throat, and he peered down at her. Verity sucked in a soft breath at the piercing brilliance of his green eyes, and she was grateful the veil hid the blush heating her cheeks. He looked startled for a moment. Then he glanced up and down the street, and at the disguised carriage parked opposite his iron gate.

James Daniel Radcliffe, the Earl of Maschelly, upon first glance, did not appear either a libertine, a dastardly reprobate, or a man so handsome, the devil clearly fashioned him to tempt women to sin. Verity thought he appeared quite ordinary in a dark, brooding manner, if somewhat unkempt. The man had outrageously answered the door himself, and as if to mock her consternation, he did so with bare feet, no jacket, his white shirt sleeves rolled to his elbows and a loosely tied cravat! Massive shoulders strained against his shirt, and his trousers indecently outlined thighs that were far too hard looking for a gentleman. The man was an aristocrat built like a dockworker.

Her cheeks went hot, her throat and belly too. How unpardonable he could make birds flutter in her stomach. A very unusual reaction, for she much preferred men who were fair and quick to laugh, those who were non-threatening in their demeanor. *Safe*. The very opposite of the man before her who loomed over six feet tall with the blackest scowl she'd ever seen on another's countenance. But it was this man her dearest friend, Lady Caroline Trenton, had advised was the perfect specimen to help Verity on the merry path of ruin. Though it wasn't ruination she sought, it was merely a possible consequence of her actions. But she would not be deterred, and she must be brave.

It was so absolutely reckless for her to be on this man's doorstep without a chaperone, no one must know she'd had the temerity to call upon the earl. Though dear Caroline had suggested a meeting with him, Verity was certain her friend did not mean for her to call on the man at his bachelor's residence, at night! So many wild and wicked rumors swirled about the earl. He was rumored to be dissolute, reckless, a gambler, a fighter, a great participant of sensual debauchery.

The Earl of Maschelly was wicked, they said.

He was not afraid of anyone, they rabidly whispered.

It was rumored a man of his nature spent his days in nothing but self-indulgence and sin, and his nights in recklessness at London's most dangerous haunts. He did not resist beauties, bedding a different Cyprian each night during the week, but no less than six on the weekend. That all sounded like balderdash to Verity's way of thinking, but he was still the man she needed. Though ruin and disgrace hovered. She needed him for her freedom, so she would never feel helpless or afraid ever again. He was the second step in reclaiming her dignity and her dreams.

She lowered her gloved hand which had been poised to beat the lion head knocker. "Lord Maschelly, I presume?"

Verity did not dare assume it was the butler who had opened the door in such a distinct state of dishabille. Indeed he would be fired immediately. She did not dare assume the butler would also possess the dark green eyes reflecting the forest after a night of rain, or it would be the butler in possession of such raven black hair and sensually full lips. He wasn't handsome in the soft manner or anything like the refined and elegant men of the *ton*. This was all hard edges and so compelling she stared helplessly, absurdly grateful he could not see that she gawked like a silly miss.

The man regarded her with a fascinated eye, then drew an audible breath. "And who the hell are you?" His tone was crisp and stinging as the lash of a whip.

She winced at his uncouthness, appalled at his lack of civility. But there was nothing she could do about that, not when she needed him. And strangely, his impertinence calmed her. "First, I apologize for calling without notice and in such a clandestine manner. It was unavoidable, since you've ignored my previous letters asking to meet discreetly. It is of the utmost importance I have a private audience with you, my lord."

"Why?"

Verity took a steadying breath. "I have a proposition for you, one that is best discussed in privacy."

His scowl went even darker. "Well hell, no one has ever offered it up on my front step before in such an obvious manner."

She gasped at the sheer effrontery of his lewd suggestion. Verity was quite aware of what he referred to, and almost turned around and departed then at his lack of gentlemanlike manners. The words were cutting and hinted at a cynicism she'd not expected.

"I am a *lady*, my lord, you will comport yourself accordingly, and what I have for you is a business proposal," she said, careful not to choke on her mortification, grateful her voice did not tremble.

Darkness and fog blanketed the area, and the few gas lamps shed little light. All that was convenient to her disguise, but she felt nervous and uncertain.

"A lady? At my home at this hour, without a chaperone?" This bit was drawled with mocking cynicism.

"Yes," she replied pertly, "I daresay a woman of my years can venture out without undue speculation and ruin." Such ridiculousness for if she was discovered, her life, and reputation would be in shambles. But Verity was desperate and afraid, and he was someone who could help her put her nightmares to rest, even if he did not know it. "And the gentlemanly conduct would be to invite me inside away from possible speculation and the dreadful chill in the air."

Those beautiful eyes stared at her veil as if he wanted to discern the features beneath the disguise. Nervous energy had her tugging at the piece of lace brushing against her chin. Then to her relief and amazement, he stepped back and bid her entrance.

Verity made her way inside, startled at the overwhelming darkness. No lamplight shone in the hallway, but she could discern enough to follow the earl to a large and tastefully furnished drawing room. A fire blazed merrily in the hearth, and the earl waved at her to sit. She lowered herself into the plush sofa, anxious that he remained standing.

"Will you also sit, my lord?"

The earl arched a brow, and it was then she noted the faint discoloring on his left cheek.

Verity became aware of the subtle scent of his sweat as he moved closer. And he walked as if hurt, a slight tilt to the left, favoring his side. The brawn of his body was overwhelming. He was tall, so much broader than she. A small part of her wanted to move away. But her courage could not falter now, not when she had reached so far. Inexplicably she felt at once both threatened and secure. Foolish to feel safe for she did not know the manner of man he was. Just what the rumors said. And she felt silly for resting her plans on the entirety of idle speculations.

"Will you need refreshment?" he demanded in that terrible uncivil way of his.

"There is no need to be boorish," she sniffed.

"I did not invite you here."

Verity flushed. "You did not, and I apologize for the intrusion. It is still not an excuse for your incivility."

"Do you wish for a drink?"

"No," she said with polite stiffness.

There was a decanter of amber liquid on the oak table before her, an empty glass, and a white handkerchief that had a suspicious red stain. She had interrupted his drinking. He poured his amber liquid into the glass, and then lowered himself into the sofa opposite her.

"What is this proposal?" he said, impatience coloring his tone.

She cleared her throat delicately, wondering where to start with her very scandalous and unorthodox request. "Society says a dance from you has the power to ruin any young lady. And perhaps that is why you've never asked anyone to the dance floor."

"And do you want ruin, do you?" his voice was a purr of sin and darkness, and some unfathomable emotion she did not understand. It had the edge of anger, causing a ripple of discomfort to course over her skin.

She took a steadying breath and met his curious gaze, ignoring his interruption. "They say you are an untested king in the underground pugilist world of London. That you made your fortune on the blood and fractured limbs of others. Those other men…lords and those common folks, admire you… revere you even. Your nose has been broken three times, your ribs cracked numerous times, yet you've never been beaten. You understand honor *and* dishonor. You are a fair man but can be dangerous when crossed. You've been the 11th Earl of Maschelly for seven years now, and the loudest rumor in the *ton* is that you are now seeking a wife, preferable an heiress, whose father has political connections to aid you in becoming the Member of Parliament for the area where your earldom is situated."

He was silent for the longest moment. Shuffling sounds crept into the still of the night, and Verity glanced around nervously. He gripped his glass, drinking deeply, his gaze never leaving her veiled expression.

"So you know something about my reputation…and you are here…alone with me. Curious. Who are you?"

She licked her lips. "I cannot own to my identity at the moment. Not until a bargain has been struck."

His stare was unnerving, intense, and quite intelligent. "What do you want?"

The words lashed at her, and she stiffened. "I… I would like you to teach me to fight, my lord."

Silence fell upon the room, and he stared at her as if he peered into her very soul. She felt exposed and vulnerable, because so much rode on his response to her simple yet unorthodox and scandalous question. A response which he refrained from giving, he only stared, taking the measure of her. Had she made an error in approaching him? Had her hopes for freedom come to a sudden premature halt?

CHAPTER 2

"To *fight*?" Incredulity colored the earl's tone.

Verity flushed and her heart jerked with more erratic force. "Yes, to fight, to defend myself."

Lord Maschelly regarded her with a surprised amusement that irked her, but she pressed on, "And in return I…I will teach you how to comport yourself as a gentleman should." She waited uncertainly for his response her heart hammering like a trapped bird.

"I am the Earl of Maschelly," he said flatly. "I am at a loss as for how you believe there is something I am lacking, and *you* would be the one to render lessons." His tone was cold, but Verity heard the hint of warning, heard the chilling distance creeping into his tone, and heard the vulnerability beneath the surface of that dark rumble.

The idea that a man who seemed so self-assured and dynamic could have any vulnerabilities startled her. She cleared her throat delicately. "There…there is a rumor that Lady Susanna, Lord Nelson's cherished daughter refused your offer of marriage because of …because…"

"He is a brute! No refined manners or sensibilities, with disgusting calluses on his palms. How can I marry such a man?" Those had been the words Susanna had cried prettily in her lace handkerchief when she'd called upon Verity last week.

"She declined your offer of courtship because you did not seem as refined as other gentlemen in the *haut monde*. There is also a rumor that…that she set certain conditions, that if you met them, she would marry you. And some of those are that…that you learn to dance and write poems."

Verity almost smiled at the outraged scowl darkening his features, noting that stubble showed on his jaw. "And her father is willing to allow her those caveats. I…I thought we could help each other," she ended shakily, not liking the desperate quality to her voice.

"You truly think I give a bloody damn about what Lady Susanna and the rest of society thinks?"

Verity gasped at his shocking profanities. "My lord, please control your tongue!"

He stared at her, clearly surprised. "I do not bend to the whim of those who believe they are my betters. If you do not like the manner of my speech, you are free to leave."

The soft contempt in his voice rattled her composure, and every touch of his eyes on her veil felt fraught with peril.

He took a drink, peering at her over the rim of the glass. After taking several sips, he said, "I do not care about the pretty little gossips you've heard about me in your drawing rooms and balls. And I cannot fathom why you believe I would help you to do anything as outlandish as learn to *fight*. Bloody hell. I am not even certain I gather your meaning or intention. I may not have mixed with your set long, but you are all about propriety and ridiculous exacting standards."

He stood, and Verity rose, clasping her hands before her middle. The posture was a defensive one, but she couldn't help it.

"I cannot help you. Now I will ask you to take your leave."

"My lord…" At first, her plan had struck her as desperate and simpleminded. But the more she'd pondered the matter, the clearer her sense of purpose became. And she'd had five long days and nights to plan her next steps. She could not rely on her brother, the Earl of Sutcliffe, to be her defender and protector. Once she had loved him dearly, as a sister ought to love her brother, but he'd not seen her as more than a nuisance, a duty to discard. The wealthier the bidder the better, if he had his way. Nor did he believe in her and defended her honor when she'd needed him the most, instead, he had threatened to commit her to a mental institution.

How she wished she could walk over to the earl, take his hands, and press the tips of his fingers to her temple and have every thought flow from her mind to his. Four years ago, when she had been a silly, idealistic eighteen-year-old debutante, a lecherous snake had attacked her. The visions of grasping hands, punishing kisses, brutal fingers digging into her thighs, the rending of her clothes churned in her thoughts. As always, the memory made her gorge rise, and she fought to hide the reaction.

That man, Marquess Durham, had not managed to rape her, but he had hurt, humiliated, and frightened Verity terribly. For four years she had hidden away from the memory and the shame of it all in Bedfordshire, to her mother and brother's relief. Somehow, she knew deep down, one of the steps in reclaiming herself was to know how to fight. It was outrageous, scandalous, bordered on the brink of madness, but she needed to do something.

Lord Maschelly set his glass down on the table with a soft *clink* and made to walk away.

"I dare because I do not want to be afraid anymore," she said softly.

And she would see the very brute who had attacked her within society. A beast her brother called a friend. A blackguard society loved and respected. The heir to a respectable and powerful dukedom. The very awareness of it made her want to vomit.

The earl froze and his arresting gaze landed on her. "And of what are you afraid?"

Of being helpless again, of having no one believe me or to defend my pride and honor. When she had fled to her brother, her clothes torn, her cheeks bruised and her lips bloodied, he hadn't demanded her attacker's name to make the man pay for his crimes.

Albert had asked one question with her mother looking on with tears in her eyes.

Can we force him to marry you?

As if what had happened had been a case of a compromising situation.

Her soul had recoiled at the repugnant notion. She'd answered no with all honesty for Durham had been recently married. They had not asked for her attacker's identity, and she had been too afraid to give it, believing his conduct to be her fault. Once she'd wanted a whirlwind courtship, a handsome beau who would woo her most ardently and then propose. She had wished for it, desired it, and hoped endlessly. Suddenly all her dreams had vanished like smoke in the wind, buried under shame, doubt, and fear.

When the marquess had attacked Verity, somehow, he'd stolen her confidence and dreams, left her guilt-ridden, and it infuriated her knowing that she had allowed it for four long years. And though her brother wanted her off his hands, it had been convenient for the family to agree for Verity to remain in the country to help nurse Aunt Imogen who had been feeling poorly for some time. *No more*. One of the steps in reclaiming herself was to be able to defend herself. Even if she would never use the knowledge, the fact that she *could*, perhaps then she would no longer scream at shadows.

"What are you afraid of?" he repeated, his tone low and curious.

"Someone…someone hurt me." It took so much to admit that when her family had made her feel at fault. "*There are consequences to youthful exuberance*," her mother had cried at one point.

Taking a deep breath, Verity repeated it, only stronger this time. "Someone hurt me."

The earl faltered into remarkable stillness, a dark expression crossing his face before his mien shuttered.

She waited in pained silence for his response.

Finally, he asked, "Do I need to summon a doctor?"

"No," she said, clearing her throat delicately. "It was some years ago."

His curious expression didn't change, and it was making her uncomfortable. "Then it is no concern of mine, lady."

How remarkably disinterested he sounded. The notion he would have aided her had been wild and farfetched. In the realms of possibilities, it was along the same ideas of dragons being real. Yet the disappointment that lodged against her stomach felt like a massive boulder, pushing her into the carpeted floor.

"I…I heard a story of how you helped Lady Morton with a delicate problem she had, and Miss Cecily Bateman. You broke Lady Morton's husband's arm for beating her most severely, and Miss Cecily's blackmailer had been persuaded to direct his nefarious attentions elsewhere. From your expression, I am assuming there is some veracity to those stories. I was hoping you would help me too. *Please*." And everyone knew that a lord had slapped his servant at Tattersall last week and Maschelly had intervened. Despite everything, he was kind. "I gambled my reputation in coming to see you."

"I am sorry you undertook the disagreeable task of coming here this late for nothing. I cannot help you."

Verity felt tears prick behind her lids, and she lifted her chin, grateful he could not see that she was on the verge of crumbling. She had been so hopeful. "May I tell you a story before I leave?"

He stared at her, a peculiar expression on his face. "Go on," he urged softly.

"Five years and eleven months ago, a young lady met a lord, a friend of her brother's, whom she believed to be good-natured and amiable. Being eighteen years at the time, she was hopeful, and wistful with dreams of a prince charming, an unmatched love, and marriage and family. So…she foolishly allowed the lord to kiss her." The memory unsettled Verity sufficiently to make her press a hand over her mouth through the veil, even though she recounted the experience from an out of body perspective.

"They took long walks in the country, rides in his curricle, and she anticipated an offer. When no offer came forth, she daringly asked what his intentions were, for she was impatient to start living the life she'd long dreamed for herself. That was when he revealed he already had a wife…who lived in Scotland with his two children. The young lady was not being courted for marriage, but to…to be his mistress. She was disconcerted, for how could such a person be a gentleman. She lashed out in anger, calling him every vile name she knew and made to depart his presence, and…and the veil of her innocence was rent from her as he attacked her. Tou…touching her in places no one should ever touch. And treating her in ways no woman nor lady should ever endure. Her Aunt came upon them, and that is how she was spared greater pain and humiliation."

The earl had clenched his hands into tight fists at his side. "And did her brother call him out and put a bullet through his black heart?"

She laughed, the sound hoarse with remembered pain. "No. That vile blackguard is the son of a duke. Somehow the young lady's brother was convinced by the attacker's story that she was the seducer and he fell under her seductive wiles. She was blamed entirely, and her brother and mother were ashamed of her."

A harsh curse slipped from Lord Maschelly.

"She was no longer the bright, rosy debutante. With all her aspirations replaced by nightmares which started that very night, she eschewed society and hid away in the country, in Bedfordshire to be precise, for she had become timid, a mouse afraid of her own shadow. And they've lasted for four years, six months, and eleven days."

Her voice cracked, and she took several steadying breaths to regain her composure. "That young lady, Lord Maschelly, is me. And five months ago, sometime after the nightmares had ceased, my isolation bore down on me. For I realized I still wanted everything I used to dream about. A loving husband, children to dote on, a charitable endeavor to support. I also missed my friends, attending balls, the theater, the opera, even the noise and smell of London I wished for. So, I ventured back into society…and the first night I saw my attacker at a ball I cast up my accounts. I thought I had moved past it, I thought I had healed, but I am *still* afraid."

"And why do you think learning to fight will suppress that fear?" he demanded gruffly, searching her veiled features intently.

"The night I saw him…last Friday to be precise, he touched me. It was so very fleeting, but I froze, then I trembled as if ill. Society does not know he is a snake who wears a charming mask."

She took an involuntary step back at the sudden fierceness in his expression. And Verity wondered at his reaction. She could only hope her honesty would pierce his earlier icy refusal.

"I jerked away from him, and he *laughed*." She closed her eyes briefly against the memory. "That night my dreams started again when I thought I'd left them in Bedfordshire. I do not want to feel helpless."

His eyes narrowed, and his mouth tightened. "Why are you telling me all this, I am a stranger."

"Because I desire your help, my lord. Please think on it." Then she turned and walked away.

"You court scandal and ruin if you go ahead

with such a scheme and society finds out. As you've said, you have a dream for a home and a family, are you willing to risk that?" His tone was measuring as if he was trying to determine her backbone.

She paused, and without shifting around, answered, "The freedom to rest without nightmares, to walk in the park without fearing what lurks behind the bushes, to attend a ball without dreading his presence, is worth *everything*, my lord."

CHAPTER 3

Someone hurt me…

Those softly spoken words had lodged themselves deep in James's heart and stirred something wicked and ugly inside of him. He felt oddly off balance. The temptation had been there to simply ask for her attacker's name and avenge her honor. It hadn't mattered that he did not know her identity, he despised those who hurt and abused people who should be protected. He had also never been the type to tolerate injustice. And somehow, she had uncovered that truth about him, trying to appeal to his softer side, except he had no softness in his heart.

Someone hurt me…

His unknown lady had departed a little over two

hours ago, and her softly whispered words of pain had already started their haunting. *Well hell, come on then…*

He took a sip of whisky, his fourth glass since she'd left, and he was nowhere close to being inebriated. A state he would welcome for it would numb the pain in his ribs. Tonight's fight had been rough, dirty, and unnecessary. He had enough wealth now to manage his estates comfortably, he did not need the fighting pits as he had a few years past. He'd stayed away for more than a year, and then he had stupidly allowed Lady Susanna's hysterical rejection to drive him to fighting, seeking its dark pleasure and the freedom of leaving the cares of the world behind.

Someone hurt me…

A hiss slipped from him as her soft entreaty rolled through him once again. It was nonsense, a lady wanting to fight. And he did not doubt her. There had been something wild and defiant in her expectations, even though her speech, carriage, and how she folded her damn hands screamed gentility. He admired her courage, but she was far too independent and bold. The *haut monde* had no use for people that were different, especially in their women. A rigid adherence to their rules was the general expectation.

Though it was conceivable that there were young ladies who dared to step out from under the restrictions their families and society dictated. His veiled lady would not survive long amongst the wolves of society with a personality like hers. She would be judged and found wanting for her unique bravery. Even now if society should learn that the son of a duke had attacked her in such a violent, disgusting manner, it would be her that would be judged and cast aside. Very much like what her brother had done. Her brother also deserved a rapier through his misguided and selfish heart. No doubt his connection to a future duke had been more important than protecting his sister's honor.

It was a wonder she'd had the courage to visit James in his home when she'd heard so much of his reputation.

I do not want to feel afraid.

And in that softly echoed statement, he'd felt a moment of affinity…a connection of sorts. There had been a time when he had been afraid of the older boys in the village who resented a future earl, pretending to be one of them—poor, hungry, and desperate for another life. James had been seven at the time, and those boys had been older by a few years. They'd attacked in droves, and he'd had no one to defend him. His father had abandoned him in his drunken grief and had deliberately set his only son to endure a harsh life without any of the privileges that came with being a future earl. James had learned very quickly how to fight and to hurt so he could have a measure of peace.

And it was that she wanted. Peace…to sleep and not have nightmares.

Who are you? The sudden need to know burned through him with alarming fierceness. What kind of lady was she? *Brave*. That answer was immediate. She exuded a fire and strength he had never seen in another woman, attested by her will to venture down such a dangerous and ruinous path. And the need to help her flamed through James. And perhaps he would take her offer to learn how to be the kind of man ladies of society required to be their husbands.

The yearning for such finer things, the acceptance into a world that he should have effortlessly belonged to blasted through him, yet something inside of him fiercely recoiled at bowing to any part of society's ridiculous expectations.

A gentleman?

What need did he have of such appellation? Yet the memory of how everyone looked at him, mistrustful as if he were a brute who did not belong to their society, was very reminiscent of his father's disdain. The memory of Lady Susanna's horrified refusal felt like acid against his skin.

Seven years amongst his society and he still did not feel as if he had a place.

James scowled, tugging at the loose cravat around his throat. It felt like a goddamn noose growing tighter and tighter with each reflection.

A gentleman.

And what made a man a gentleman? He peered down at his fist, wincing at the callouses and spidery network of old fighting cuts and fresh bruises.

And she believed she could help refine his hard edges more, did she? It wasn't an equitable bargain at all, but he was still tempted. For he did wish to marry and secure his heir for the earldom. He had fought too long and brutally, done so many things to save his estates to leave it all to chance. It had been his plan for several months now, and he had been foolish to invest his attention in a lady who only saw him as a hulking brute. The same way his father had seen him, for it had been James's size upon birth which had taken his mother's life, and his father never once let him forget it.

If this lady could help him refine those sharp edges, just perhaps they could strike a bargain. But what kind of man would merrily help a young lady of society on the path to ruin? For there was no other outcome if she persisted on such a path.

A *lady* learning to fight.

James scoffed, he considered, and his curious fascination grew in unchecked leaps and bounds. Women were amongst the most vulnerable in society. So they should be the most protected, but what if by way of indifference, selfishness, or lack of family they were not protected?

In such a case James could affirm the confidence that one gains from being able to defend oneself. There was logic in her reasoning. But what of her reputation? Though degrees of ruination and respectability were solely ascribed by those with elevated opinions of the *haut monde*. When in truth, neither the lady's virtue nor character would be sullied. And it seemed she was of a similar leaning in placing little stock in the *ton's* opinions. James very soon became reconciled to the notion of assisting her, for he truly hated the helplessness which had echoed in her voice.

But where to find her? The foolish woman had not thought to leave a card or any clues to her identity that he could pursue. Is it that she planned to pay him another clandestine nighttime visit? Making an impulsive decision, he surged to his feet and faltered at the naked woman draped in the doorway.

Bloody hell, he forgot she awaited him in his chamber upstairs, and a woman like Countess Marissa Michaels was not to be ignored and forgotten.

"Darling, I actually fell asleep waiting," she said with a small pout, meant to be enticing.

James suddenly felt tired of the games that were an intricate part of his lifestyle. Shame and anger also burned through him in equal measure. The Countess was married, and he'd promised himself years ago never to take a married woman to his bed. Simply because he believed in the sanctity of some vows. And a marriage, promising to be faithful to each other's body, desires, hopes and dreams, that felt like something worth protecting. While he'd felt the awful sting from the brutal rejection of his father, James had weirdly admired the man's dedication to his beloved countess. He had grieved her until the end of his days.

It seemed his unknown lady had saved him from a folly he shouldn't have needed rescuing from. James set his glass down on the table and prowled over to the countess. With a smile, she tossed her curly mane of blonde hair, allowed the dark blue silken robe to part perfectly down the middle, revealing her delectable body, hinting at the wild night of passion that could be spent between her legs.

James's mind or body did not stir, and he belatedly realized perhaps he hadn't needed rescuing. And that he had lingered in the library drinking, even though a woman willing to indulge in debauchery had awaited him in his chamber.

"Forgive me, Marissa," he said with a rueful smile upon reaching her. He lightly touched her cheek with the back of his hand, not wanting to abrade her skin with his rough callouses. "You are a lovely woman, but you should not be here. I will arrange for you to be discreetly taken home to your lord."

Her blue eyes spat fire before narrowing. "Who is she?"

He swallowed back the sigh of impatience. "Marissa—"

"I heard voices. A woman's one. I saw from the

upstairs window as she left, and I waited for you to come up to me. Who is she?"

James lowered his hand. "No one of your concern. She has nothing to do with me realizing this is a mistake. Now let me take you home."

Her eyes searched his and then she sighed. "We will not have an *affaire de coeur*, will we?"

"No," he said with another smile to lessen the sting. "It was a moment of insanity which passed before we both did something foolish."

"I am entirely aware of what I wanted to do… of what I still want to do," she purred, running a finger over his bottom lip.

His lack of reaction was quite evident, and with a disdainful sniff, she twirled around and marched away from him. Almost an hour later the lady was finally presentable and ready to depart. James arranged for a carriage to take her home, but she haughtily informed him that she would be going to Lady Trenton's ball. He bid her good evening, had his valet draw a bath, and soaked his bruised body for a very long time before retiring to bed.

Shortly after dawn, he finally abandoned bed to call upon his good friend Viscount Shaw who resided in Mayfair with his lovely viscountess. The butler delivered James to a drawing room with a lit fire and then went to summon his master.

They had met in one of the many fighting pits that peppered London. Not the fancy places like Gentleman Jackson's, but those rings where men laid bets on the outcome of a fight as if they were in a gambling den. Many lords trained at Gentleman Jackson's and took their skills to the underground ring—where fighters did not follow the London Prize Ring rules, hoping to make enough money to pay off their debts or become solvent again. Many did not find honor in it, for it was raw and gritty, the blood and the pain a reality that was hard to shy from. James had been desperate years ago when he had taken to those rings, and those rings had given him money, a backbone made of steel, many cuts and bruises, and lasting friendships he had never thought he would find. For a time, many had also referred to him as the bare-knuckle king for never losing a bout.

Almost half an hour later, the drawing room door was pushed open and Sebastian Rutledge, Viscount Shaw strolled inside. The man did not look pleased to see him.

James stood, tugged off his gloves, dipped into

his pocket for two thin leather straps and started to bind his hands.

Sebastian scowled. "You pulled me from the wonderful warmth of my wife's arms for a bout of boxing at 6 a.m.?" he growled, looking ready to knock out James's light.

"And also for a spot of conversation." He paused on a sigh. "You are normally an early riser, and I need...I need a round. My mind could not quiet."

"I heard you went to The Club only last evening and had a prizefighting match with Lord Barton."

The Club, as everyone referred to the gambling den owned by Viscount Worsley, another lord who stood on the edges of acceptance because of the manner in which he had made his money. At the back of the gambling halls, there was a room solely dedicated to prizefighting matches. When James climbed into the ring last night, the crowd had been pleased one of its bare-knuckle kings had returned after so long. The fight had been vicious and had lasted several rounds. James's satisfaction had been hollow, and he had been mildly shocked by how much Lady Susanna's rejection had affected his composure. "It did not suffice."

"So you won then?"

He had won the match and a purse of six thousand pounds. "I did."

Sebastian considered him for a few seconds then nodded.

James grunted, stripping from his jacket while moving toward a room in the viscount's townhouse dedicated to sparring. Soft footfalls and muttered curses followed, and James smiled, feeling quite pleased to be lucky in a friendship with a man who enjoyed a good bout of boxing just as much as he did.

A few moments later, they circled each other, dancing and weaving with ease.

"What happened?" Shaw asked. "It is unlike you to show up without announcing. God knows you've tried to be very proper and exact even with friends."

James ignored the jibe that he had tried to be an ideal gentleman and was ridiculous at it. "I had an unexpected visitor. A woman at my home a few hours ago."

"You visited to provide the details of an interlude?" Sebastian asked with a jab toward his midsection.

James danced out of his friend's reach, bobbed, and slammed his fist into his side.

"My wife will not take kindly to any bruises on me, and my Fanny can be quite fierce."

He grinned and before James could shift away, Sebastian delivered a nice slam to his side. With a grunt, James backed away, liking that he was working up a sweat, that his muscles were already burning, and that primal need shifted through his system.

"Are you familiar with a lady who has been away from society these last four seasons, but has resurfaced, say, about the last five to six months?"

Sebastian faltered and stared at him with a measure of surprise. "Well, that was very precise."

"A lady fitting that description came to me, in disguise, with a very peculiar request."

An eyebrow winged upward. "Which is?"

James hesitated slightly. "To teach her to fight, to defend herself."

Sebastian smiled. "You do know I teach my wife how to fight. My factories are in rough areas of London, and she insists on visiting me at times. With the conditions as they are, many justifiably angry workers and the union-encouraged strikes which lead to rioting, I have taught her to fight. I daresay with the right incentive my Fanny can lay you flat on your rear, Maschelly."

This was said with a good deal of pride and admiration for his viscountess. But James already knew his friend's lady had the courage of a lion. Only last year she had jilted a powerful lord and left the dishonorable bounder at the altar. She had done that, knowing the scandal that would forever be attached to her name. That showed a strength of character that was rare, and more than once James had thought how lucky his friend was in his choice of partner.

Sebastian continued, "And the sport is an excellent exercise for young ladies, the general thought is that it keeps them fit and healthy. And I know many take lessons at their home."

"I assure you it is not those gentle lessons she seeks." He thought of his veiled lady. "For her, it would not be a form of exercise."

"Are you certain?"

"Yes. Someone hurt her, and she needs this to feel safe again. I suspect everyone who should have protected the lady disappointed her, and she now feels she can rely on no one but her own ingenuity and strength."

"It sounds as if you admire the lady," Sebastian observed.

"I do in some fashion, but I refused her."

"But you've since changed your mind?" Sebastian asked archly, and with some amusement. "And here I thought the wickedest earl in London was trying to be *proper*…a gentleman. How odd you would willingly help a lady to ruin, casting yourself in more negativity for the vultures."

James grunted. "Do you have any notion of who she could be? A young lady who has been away for the last four seasons, and only recently returned to town? I cannot fathom there could be several such ladies."

"I will ask my dear Fanny. You know I am not up to date on the latest *on dits*. My wife though seems to be too aware of most of the *ton's* business. And I am delightfully obliged to listen when she imparts all the news."

And that would have to do. "Please tell your viscountess I would appreciate any insight she could offer."

"Did you receive an invitation to Lady Springfield's ball?"

James usually ignored most of the invitations sent to his home, especially the frivolous variety. This had been the first season he had tried to dip his toes into the tricky waters of the *ton* to net himself a lady of quality. Foolish of him to believe a young lady would appreciate his checkered past. His title and wealth seemed to have little meaning to the one lady who had caught his fancy. He was not quite refined enough for her sensibilities. Now he couldn't stop thinking that many, if not all, ladies would have a similar opinion. *A gentleman*. What had Lady Susanna accused him of tearily when she'd rejected his suit? Ah yes, he had never asked her to dance, nor had he written her poems, or personally delivered flowers. James scowled recalling her hysterical nonsense. "How is Lady Springfield's ball relevant?"

"The Countess likes scandal and anything society deems as too wicked, so I am sure she sent you one."

"I am assuming you have a point."

"According to my lovely wife, everyone who's anyone will be at Lady Springfield's ball tonight. Perhaps your mysterious lady will be present."

James felt bewildered at the waves of anticipation that buffeted him. "Then I shall endeavor to be there."

They resumed their friendly sparring, and almost an hour later, James departed and made his way home. He headed straight to his chamber, the weight of the evening before—the sleepless night, and his sparring settling on his shoulder like a boulder. He removed all his clothing and unmentionables until he was naked, then he dropped himself onto his bed with a deep groan of relief. Sleep beckoned, and for the first time in a long time, he felt a sense of profound anticipation at attending a ball.

CHAPTER 4

"You retired early from Lady Balfour's ball last evening," Albert, Earl of Sutcliffe, and Verity's brother said in a very disagreeable tone. "Lord Aldridge was considerably disappointed he'd not been able to dance the supper waltz with you."

"I had a headache and had to leave. Surely mamma informed you?" Verity said, spreading strawberry preserves atop her bread.

Their mother took a delicate sip of her tea, before speaking. "I did inform your brother, he is determined to be contrary. And, my dear, you missed an excessively diverting evening."

"You left within half an hour of arriving," Albert said. "What did you do upon arriving home?"

For a wild moment, she wondered if he knew of her clandestine activities. Surely not? For then there would have been threats of banishment to the country, or God forbid, to a mental house. "I find it quite odd you need the details of my evening, Albert. But if you must know, after having a few relaxing cups of tea, I had a very agreeable evening reading," she said with a polite smile.

Her brother nodded as if he approved heartily as to how she spent her time. "You'll rest and ensure you come with mamma and me to Lady Springfield's ball tonight. Viscount Aldridge is interested in courting you, he made his sentiments known to me."

Verity stared at her brother for several moments. "I am three and twenty, Albert. I am quite able to decide on a gentleman I am comfortable with for marriage. Lord Aldridge does not suit my temperament, and I am certain he could not be interested in me since we have never spoken beyond polite queries about the weather."

Her brother slammed his fist on the table, startling her. "You will listen—" Albert broke off, controlling himself with a visible effort, setting his teeth. "I am only doing what is best for you, Verity. He has an estate in Berkshire, and in Kent. His income is twenty thousand a year, and I have seen how he admires you. It is prudent to give the viscount a chance, and I'll not allow any silly excuses for you. You are three and twenty, and it is time you live on another's benevolence."

She dabbed her lips with a serviette, trying to control the anger twisting through her. "The viscount is…he is friends with the marquess. I could not endure such a connection, nor will I pretend to."

Verity did not need to name him. It lingered in the air…*the marquess who attacked and hurt me.*

A grimace of anger crossed her brother's face. He did not like whenever Verity mentioned the "distasteful incident," the sobriquet he'd applied to her greatest shame and pain.

"We have agreed to leave that distasteful in—"

"In Bedfordshire, I know. So you and mamma repeatedly inform me with little regards to my feelings and well-being."

"Verity!" her mother scolded, disapproval crinkling the lines at her mouth. "There is no need to castigate your brother. We are supporting you in not speaking of your behavior and how it almost ruined a connection with Lord—"

"Do not speak his name!" She tried to steady

her voice. In another moment she would be weeping, she realized with panic. It would kill something inside of her if they realized how much the entire dreadful encounter still scared and pained her. Not when they had not cared. Not when they cared more about their connections in the *ton* than her safety and happiness. Not when they held no belief in her honor. "If you will excuse me."

She pushed her chair back, stood, and sedately made her way from the breakfast room before she did something shocking like throwing the dish of strawberry preserves into her brother's face. Pausing, she turned around and lifted her chin. "Father would have been abjectly ashamed of both of you for he would never have permitted anyone to escape the consequences of such vile actions." There, before she'd not have the courage to say it to their faces.

Her mother called her name, and Verity pretended not to hear the admonition. She made her way to her room and over to her writing desk. There she lowered herself into a chair and reached into the small drawer for a sheaf of paper. She would pen a letter to the earl, but what could she say? She had already revealed so much of her fears and vulnerabilities to a man she did not know. The awareness had left her sleep troubled, an unknown desperation lodged inside her heart.

Tonight, she would see Marquess Durham. Bile rose in her throat. *Courage*, Verity, she reminded herself. They were of the same society, and she had to learn how to be in the vile cur's presence without fighting the urge to cast up her accounts.

A knock sounded, and her lady's maid Anna entered. "The Duchess of Carlyle has called for you, my lady."

A swift rush of pleasure claimed Verity, and she forgot about writing a letter to plead with the earl. She and the Duchess had only become friends recently, after the scandal which had blasted through the *ton* just a few months past. Miss Pippa Cavanaugh, now the Duchess of Carlyle, had been a notorious gossip columnist who had snared herself one of society's beloved dukes. Society had been a party to their love affair as some of their laundry had been aired in the newspapers to the delight of the *ton*.

The couple had been infamous, and even her mother had scrambled to invite the duke and duchess of Carlyle to their dinner parties and intimate circles. It was at Lady Somerton's ball however Verity had made Pippa's acquaintance.

Verity had informed the new duchess how much her courage had inspired her, and they had become close. It was a friendship Verity treasured. She quickly changed into a more presentable gown, a light blue plaid taffeta dress, with its tight waist and elegant ruffled elbow-length sleeves.

Verity then made her way to the drawing room where the duchess awaited her. Pippa lowered her teacup when Verity entered and smiled brightly. The Duchess was draped in a dark yellow gown which flattered her curvaceous figure to its best advantage. Her dark hair was fashioned in an intricate chignon and several strands of lustrous pearls encircled her neck, with matching ear bobs.

"How did last night go?" she asked archly without indulging in any pleasantries.

Verity had been comfortable in confiding her plans to Pippa, and the duchess had been present at tea when Lady Caroline had named the earl as the gentleman to help Verity.

She laughed softly, even if without humor. She lowered herself beside the duchess on the sofa and shifted slightly, so they faced each other. "Disastrous. The earl refused. But I was not seen, and my family believes I spent the evening in my room with a book."

Her gray eyes went soft with sympathy. "Oh Verity, I am terribly sorry. The notion had been hare-brained, but I did so hope for your sake he would agree."

She leaned forward and poured herself another cup of tea from the service trolley. "My brother also seems determined to hand me off to Viscount Aldridge, a man whom I've no affection for. I do wish to marry and move away from this dreadful family, but I would like my husband to be my own choice."

Pippa frowned. "I've every reason to believe that Viscount Aldridge is a fortune-hunter, and I should speculate on it and warn this season's crop of fresh debutantes," said the duchess. "The viscount and his younger brothers are notorious for their profligacy. I am at a loss as to why your brother would think such a match suitable! I daresay the viscount is after your inheritance."

Her eyes held a great deal of intelligence as she stared at Verity. "What will you do?"

"About the Lord Maschelly or Lord Aldridge?"

The duchess popped a piece of cake and chewed thoughtfully before answering, "Both."

"I will not marry Lord Aldridge even if they drag me kicking and screaming to the altar. I know who I want to marry. Not his name, but his character. Someone kind and gentle. Protective. Safe. A man who does not make me feel threatened."

An image of the earl's brawn and the peculiar heat she'd felt upon looking at him brought a surge of discomfort through Verity. Oddly she hadn't felt frightened in his presence, more of an awareness of his male appeal.

"As for the earl, perhaps I will be able to find myself another lord to assist."

"I suppose there is more than one wicked rogue that could be convinced of your madness," Pippa said.

The idea had been to approach a man on the fringe of society's good graces, one wicked and scandalous enough that he would not care she was breaking the rules of propriety. He wouldn't care that she was being reckless and independent. He wouldn't care that she was trying to be bold. But he would have enough honor not to take advantage of her pain and need to learn. Only the earl of Maschelly had seemed to fit the type of man she needed.

"Unfortunately, no one else will do. Perhaps I

will have to find another way to entice him to render aid."

Pippa arched a brow. "I am all ears."

Except she had no notion how to convince him. Frustrated Verity cried, "Perhaps I shall offer him kisses instead of lessons of etiquette. Isn't he London's wickedest earl? Perhaps I offered the wrong incentive!"

The duchess dissolved into a peal of laughter, and it was so carefree and unconcerned with decorum, Verity smiled. "I suppose it does seem a trifle unreasonable."

"Only unreasonable?" the duchess asked with a twinkle in her eyes. "I cannot help think you found Lord Maschelly interesting."

More like compelling. But Verity did not say so, instead deftly shifting the topic. "Will you be at Lady Springfield's ball later on? My brother has demanded my presence, and I fear I cannot plead a headache again. Your presence will surely enliven my boredom greatly." And perhaps aid Verity in keeping her sanity if she should encounter the marquess.

"I shall be there," Pippa said.

And a tension Verity hadn't been quite aware of lifted from her shoulders. She would attend this ball and have a jolly good time. She'd not let memories of that vile snake steal any more enjoyment from her life. However, Verity would be cautious and ensure she stayed close to her friends for the night.

※

It was his veiled lady indeed.

Sebastian had indicated this young lady, saying Fanny had known of only one person to fit the circumstances he'd described—a Lady Verity, whose family held the Earldom of Sutcliffe. Staring at her now, James recognized her with little effort. He was certain this young lady in the beautiful icy blue ballgown with pearls seeded in the hems, a charmingly lowered décolletage, and tiny puffed sleeves was truly her.

Though he could not see her face, how she moved, slow and graceful; the way she spoke with her hands, delicate, fluttery movements revealed her to him, for such mannerism reflected those of the lady who had visited him. The shape and size were also entirely accurate. She appeared a petite, fragile-looking young woman with a head of the richest darkest hair he'd ever beheld. She was apparently a lady of excellent breeding with a sensuality that was unstudied and quite appealing. James watched her discreetly from his position on the balcony of the upper floor drowning out the idle chatter and laughter around him.

A man approached her, and she stiffened. The smile of her lips appeared strained to James even at this distance. But then she laughed, and he frowned. The lady dipped into a curtsy, and a few moments later she was on the dance floor with the man. She was the embodiment of grace and elegance as the man twirled her into a waltz.

An unfathomable need to be the one dancing with her arrowed through his heart. He smiled slightly without humor. He was a bumbling oaf when he tried to dance. The few lessons he had dared to take several months ago would not have him moving with such grace as those dandies on the floor.

An undeniable curiosity rose within him as he watched her. She seemed so at ease in the crush, not how he imagined someone who had been away for four years would appear. *Is it truly you, Lady Verity?* The dance ended, and he moved through the crowd, drifting closer to her. His mysterious lady collected a glass of champagne from a passing footman, and sipped. The lady shifted, and their gazes collided. The last remnants of his uncertainty died. This was the woman who had visited last night. Her lips parted on a gasp, and her eyes widened with recognition, hope, and oddly, panic. Clearly, she did not expect any form of social interaction between them, only clandestine meetings.

This close, he noted her finely molded cheekbones were slightly high, her skin creamy and glowing with health, her lips generous and soft. There was a stubborn pride in the set of her small chin, and her eyes were the brownest he'd ever seen. Her lovely eyes were under delicately arched brows, and her generous mouth seemed to be made for smiling and perhaps kissing. Faintly shocked at his errant thought, he glanced away briefly. His eyes traveling over the many people at Lady Springfield's townhouse, every public room, garden, and terrace seemed to be overflowing with guests.

When he looked back to her, the lady was pushing through the crowded ballroom with deft ease. At the edge of the hall, she paused, turned toward him, and stared at him for several unblinking moments. There was a clear invitation he should follow. James made his way in her direction, leisurely, ensuring no one paid too much attention to him, though it was quite unlikely with the number of people crammed into the ballroom.

James exited in time to see the tail of her gown disappearing around a corner. He made his way down the hallway, passed a few guests, and made a similar left turn. She was not in sight, but then he spied a door which had been left discreetly open. James made his way to it, pushed the door wider and stepped inside.

"Close it," she commanded huskily.

Something unknown surged through him, and the sensations were so baffling he took a few seconds to comply. She was being impetuous, shortsighted to risk them being alone in such a place. The scandal, if they were seen closeted away, would be horrendous for her. James was used to the endless speculations into his life, and the various sobriquets of wicked and dissolute.

However, he closed the door with a soft *snick*. A merry light danced from the fireplace, and a lamp was lit in what appeared to be a small parlor. The heavy drapes were also drawn, revealing a garden by the windows.

"Why are you here?"

"I was invited."

"Balls are not your haunting ground, Lord

Maschelly. That is commonly known," she retorted, clasping her hands before her middle. A nervous and telling gesture.

The lady was charming indeed. She was short, lushly curved and quite petite, and the top of her head would barely reach his shoulder. And it bemused him that he would like to kiss her. She inspired wicked fantasies of tangled limbs atop silken sheets, and he felt like a cad for having the provocative thoughts.

He wanted to move closer but knew he would be like a hulking beast beside her sweet, delicate femininity. With a scowl, he glanced down at his large hands. Possibly even scare her, for now, she looked at him with wary determination. James must never forget she had survived an attack which still haunted her. She had a deceptive air of fragility, but he saw the core strength staring back at him.

"Who are you?"

"Lady Verity Ayles, sister to Lord Sutcliffe," she said with a lift of her chin. "Though I suspect you are aware of my identity. I ask, my lord, again, why are you here?"

He knew the earl. Sutcliffe visited the club often enough to gamble and tumble with the sought-after

Cyprians which visited each night, searching for their next wealthy protector.

He recalled the earl was young, eager to please those more powerful than himself, and ill-equipped to be the head of his family. A few nights ago, he had been at the club with the Marquess of Durham. The earl had laughed loudly at everything the marquess said, and from what James had overheard, the man had little in the way of humorous anecdotes. He bragged of seducing debutantes and married women, hardly something to be proud of.

"I attended the ball to find you, Lady Verity."

She inhaled sharply and stepped toward him. Her expressive eyes danced over his face, and the light of hope inside them made his throat close for a few seconds.

"Because?"

"I will teach you to fight."

***

"You can open your eyes," the earl said, his voice rich with amusement.

With a gasp, her lids flew open, and a hand fluttered to her chest. Verity hadn't realized she had closed them in profound relief. "My lord, I—"

"I'll help you."

"You are absolutely certain of this?"

"Yes."

"Why? I…no, please, you do not have to answer that, my lord. At least not now. Please know I am deeply grateful."

He looked away as if uncomfortable with her gratitude. "I will also accept your guidance in learning to be…more refined. Perhaps you will permit me to ask you for a dance after a few lessons."

She stared at him, flustered. One of the curious rumors about the earl was that he never danced. There had been much speculation to why, and now he would ask her? "The whispers from such an unprecedented action will be very loud, my lord. Nor do I think Lady Susanna would be too thrilled when you've never danced with her before."

A smile tugged at his lips. "I am no longer interested in courting Lady Susanna."

Verity stared at him in dismay. "But I believed you loved her, my lord!"

He arched a surprised brow. "Loved? Those were not the sentiments which had moved me to make an offer. The lady has made her position known and I have moved on. But I will appreciate your lessons since I still have the desire to marry eventually. And it is clear any lady of quality will appreciate a man more once he has more charming and refined sensibilities."

Mocking humor danced in his eyes at this. Yet she sensed the rejection had cut deeply. It jolted her that she wanted to know more about him and the life he had experienced which had placed that wicked cut above his brow, and the faint cynicism in his expression.

"A tutor may be the best person to guide you in the proper steps for the various dances," she said.

He moved slowly, deliberately, almost leisurely toward her, and her heart kicked a furious rhythm. Verity did not think it was fear, but a very unwelcomed and perplexing attraction to the man before her. The eyes that stared at her so unflinchingly were as deep and unfathomable as the night sky, and she felt uncomfortable in her admiration.

"A tutor could also guide you in the art of pugilism, my lady, but here we are forming a bargain to which I have one condition."

She stiffened. "Which is?"

"Sometime in the future, you will inform me of the name of your attacker."

She was suddenly aware of an aura of ruthlessness surrounding him that frightened her. Did he want to defend her honor? Verity felt bewildered, awkward, and filled with a strange sense of wonder. Her own family had not cared about her honor, why would this stranger? The words hovered on her lips, but she could not voice the questions. It felt too intimate to ask.

"I will never do anything to make you uncomfortable. Nor will I ever hurt you. I would ask for honesty between us at all times, so we do not make missteps with each other. Our…relationship is very unorthodox and quite new for me, but I do not wish to muck it up, either for you or myself."

Inexplicably, she believed him.

"Are we in agreement, Lady Verity?" he asked, unruffled by her silence.

"Yes," she murmured shakily. Verity stuck out her hand and was surprised when he shook it. "And I thank you, my lord. I shall never forget your kindness."

He smiled. It seemed terribly intimate to Verity and she was struck by the incredible sensual beauty of it. Dear God, it was dangerous to be in this man's presence, and she had struck a bargain that would allow many clandestine meetings. She blushed, and his gaze caressed over her evidently flushed cheeks.

"I should return inside. I do not wish to be missed."

"Then go. I shall send instructions to you in a letter, very discreetly."

Oddly, her feet remained rooted when she was caught in a storm of sorts. The air became heavy with a promise she did not understand, and it was then she realized he still held her hands. Slowly she pulled away, and he released her. "I…I shall look forward to it."

Something far too elusive for her to understand shifted in his beautiful eyes.

Verity turned and opened the door, slipping into the hallway, conscious of the way his eyes touched every part of her. A dangerous thrill burst in her heart, and it took every lesson in discipline she'd ever had to not turn around. Verity knew he would be hovering in the dark shadow of the doorway, watching her…and somehow, she knew his expression would not be one of serene contemplation. But one of want and need. Her heart tripped and butterflies wreaked havoc with her stomach.

She could feel way down inside of her, every nuance of his stare. An aching, terrifying awareness that he was possibly attracted to her, filled Verity's heart. And that she too…could possibly be attracted to his compelling masculinity. She closed her eyes against the very idea: he was not the ideal man for her, in any fashion. His edges were too rough, and even if she came at him with an etiquette mallet and all her knowledge of gentlemanly behavior, he would always have that dangerous aura that would scare her witless.

Dear God, have I gone too far?

CHAPTER 5

Almost a week later, on a very particular Tuesday, Verity was admitted to Lord Maschelly's townhouse, under the banner of secrecy and a pale moonlight. The butler promptly and with no fuss or frown directed her to an excessively large room with hardwood floors, bare of all furniture except a long sofa flushed against the wall below a set of French windows. A sense of unreality suffused Verity to know this was happening. The last several days had been spent in an agony of half dread and half hope. Somehow, she had expected that the earl would rescind their bargain. But he had been true to his promise and had sent very explicit arrangements the day after she'd seen him at Lady Springfield's ball.

She was to visit his townhouse three nights per week in disguise. For two nights, he would teach her about fighting, and one session would be her teaching whatever insight she held on refinement and gentility. He would send an unmarked carriage for her every Monday, Tuesday, and Thursday evenings by eight pm. It was less likely there would be any notable ball or events to happen on those days, and if there were any, she would need to be inventive and escape their confines. He would be the one to send the carriage with a coachman he trusted, and that should mitigate the chance of discovery. Verity had felt embarrassed for having not thought so far ahead.

It would have been impossible to summon her brother's carriage to take her to clandestine meetings three days a week without him discovering it. The servants were loyal to him and would have felt obliged to inform her brother of her shenanigans.

She would meet this coachman at the mews behind her townhouse. She should dress simply, in servant garb if she could, and slip through the kitchen's back entrance to lessen any chance of discovery. Of course, all this would be accomplished once her mother and brother had ventured out for the evening.

Luckily her brother had gone to his club tonight, and from experience he would not be home until well into the morning of the next day. Her mother had retired to bed early, and there was no occasion she would visit Verity's room. They were not close, at least not since the "distasteful incident." But Verity had still pushed several cushions under the blankets on her bed, and at a cursory inspection it might pass for her sleeping form.

"You are to change into that clothing," the butler said mildly, indicating the neatly folded pile on the sofa. "A young maid, Grace will assist whenever you are here, my lady. She will escort you to your chamber and attend you there. When you are finished, please see yourself back to this room. My lord will be with you shortly."

An odd warmth suffused her. Lord Maschelly had thought to provide her a lady's maid, and a chamber. It seemed the man had thought of everything.

"Thank you," she said warmly to the butler.

His eyes lingered briefly on the veil, he bowed,

then melted away as if such encounters were ordinary.

A young girl of about sixteen years entered shortly, bobbed, and said, "I'm Grace, milady. Milord said I'm to assist you in any way you wish."

"Thank you, Grace. Could you take me to my room so we may prepare?"

Verity took up the folded clothes and followed the girl from the room, down the long hallway, and then up the winding staircase to a chamber. It was a very elegant room done in brocaded blue and silver flowered wallpaper, a large four poster bed dominated the room, and a chaise longue rested close to the dancing fireplace. The room felt warm and inviting, and smelled like roses.

Soon her gown, chemise, corset and laces, and pantaloons were removed, and Verity was dressed in men's clothing. The shock of it had almost stolen her breath. Grace had assisted her in binding her breasts, until to Verity's mind, she could pass as a young lad. Then she had donned a fitted white shirt, a dark brown waistcoat, and black jacket and trousers. The trousers clung to her frame a bit too snugly, but the jacket fit perfectly. Next a white muslin cravat was tied around her throat. Atop her head, a short dark wig was fitted with pins.

Verity belatedly realized that she was dressed as a fashionable young gentleman, and as she stared at her reflection in the cheval mirror in the room, she laughed. All sense of her identity had been suppressed, and a pretty but dignified dandy stared back at her. Grace seemed pleased with her work.

"My lord is waiting for you, milady."

Verity nodded and made her way down the stairs, and to the large exercise room. There the earl waited, similarly dressed in dark evening clothes-black jacket and trousers, white undershirt, a silver waistcoat, and an expertly tied cravat. The man even had on a top hat and a cane.

"My lord," she murmured, then attempted to clear the huskiness away.

Admiration flashed in his eyes. "You make a credible young man."

The pit of her stomach felt strange and fluttery. "I gather we are not starting our lessons tonight?"

He came toward her. "What do you expect?"

She searched for the hidden meaning in the cool expression staring at her. "To learn to fight."

"And what does that mean, Lady Verity? To learn how to form a fist? Punch someone? Know when to retreat and run if necessary?"

Perhaps. "Yes." A blush warmed her skin at her naivety.

"As like most young ladies of the *ton*, I gather you have been cosseted most of your life. Have you ever seen someone fight?"

"No, of course not," she said in a horrified tone.

"Tonight, I am taking you to a club."

"A gentlemen's club!" she gasped. "My lord… that…that is simply too—" she objected, considerably surprised.

"Improper, outrageous?" he demanded with a mocking smile. "I assure you I am still a bit perturbed by our arrangement."

Casting him a glance of acute suspicion, Verity asked, "What is at this club?"

"Fighting. Many gentlemen have never been in a fight. They may have learned fencing, and perhaps even boxing. But never real fisticuffs—the kind that draws blood, and hurt, the kind that is necessary to protect dignity and life. When footpads accost them, or anyone else they freeze, and they are taken advantage of badly. You, my lady, are even more ignorant and naive when it comes to what is expected when accosted."

The truth of his words hammered at her, and memories of how helpless she had been as the marquess pinned her to the earth with his large frame and ripped at her dress made her tremble.

"I take you to the club tonight simply to open your eyes and prepare your mind. If after tonight you wish to continue…then we will."

Verity stared at the earl, equally shocked and enthralled. Learning to fight had been an idea borne of desperation, which had sounded powerfully freeing. A fighter seemed like one who was courageous, and would not fear a simple outing, or being in the same room with an odious bully. She had not honestly thought of the rudiments, or truly, even fighting herself. Somehow learning had become a symbol: to show she was once again courageous, and the witty, freedom-loving girl she had once been. But what if she were truly called upon to use her skills? The very idea made Verity feel faint and desperately afraid. And that made her angry for she was tired of feeling fear. "Take me," she murmured, lifting her eyes to meet his.

His gaze glittered with admiration and it made her feel warm inside. The earl said nothing more but led the way outside to a waiting carriage. They entered, and she sat opposite him and folded her hands in her laps. She closed her eyes briefly, an awareness of her life altering persistently buffeting her senses. Then she smiled. *Only forward, Verity…and with courage*.

Words her father had said many times to her over the years, especially as she had learned to ride horses, for she had been afraid of the animals. Words her nightmares had obscured for too long. How patient and loving her papa had been. How encouraging. She took his words, wrapped them in her heart and whispered, "And with courage, papa, I promise it."

※

LADY VERITY SMOOTHED her palms over her thighs once more, a nervous gesture she had repeated at least five times. James had no words of comfort to offer, and he leaned back against the squabs as the carriage rumbled over the cobbled streets of London to their destination. He hadn't believed she would dare show up for their lessons. That was why he had deliberately informed her of their first meeting a week in advance, enough time for her nerves to desert her, and for the lady to rethink her decision.

Most, if not all, young ladies were ruthlessly

groomed to believe in adhering to the strict and proper rules governing polite society. For an unmarried society girl, any suggestions of unique individuality were frowned upon. Yet this lady had the audacity to do so…and he admired her for it. Ardently. The awareness pulled a smile to his lips and an odd lightness lifted his heart.

Not for the first time, James wondered if he was doing the smart thing in taking her to the club. While she was not the typical, wilting, hysterical miss, she was a lady of quality. Tonight would distress her sensibilities. Yet he wanted her to understand the stark reality of what she sought. Understand the risks, the consequences, the violence, and the raw emotions of guilt and acceptance that came with lifting a fist to someone else. Whether in attack or defense, it took a different kind of strength to follow through.

"There is a rumor that you made your fortune in the fighting pits," she said unexpectedly.

James observed the fright in her eyes, and realized she wanted conversation of some sort to calm her nerves. For a moment he felt flummoxed. Most of the discourse he had with ladies of society were quite bland, uninspired, and was scripted by etiquette and an elevated sense of what was proper and just. This was not such a question. He found her forwardness refreshing, though, given their circumstance he couldn't expect differently. Even if she only sought to ease her nerves. He wanted to relieve her anxiety. It made him feel contemplative. Tenderness, that most alien and disconcerting of emotions, swelled and roiled through James. "I did make some of my wealth in that manner. The gambling tables and a few investments also helped."

"You are an earl," she said with a soft sideways glance.

"That I am, Lady Verity."

"How did an earl end up with a reputation as one of London's fiercest fighters? It is most unusual." At his silence she continued, "If you do not mind my curiosity?"

He'd done what he had to do to save his family: the tenant workers of his land whom he had grown up with, the servants of the house who had pooled their monies together to buy him books, boots in winter, because his father had not given a damn. When he'd inherited the lands and four estates, there hadn't been money to invest in the latest farming techniques and equipment. Many had stood to lose their livelihood and homes they had lived in for years.

"It had been necessary."

"Your earldom was impoverished?"

"My father died seven years ago when I was one and twenty. Upon claiming my inheritance, the lawyers informed me my coffers were empty, and a few of the estates heavily burdened by debts and mortgages."

"That must have been terrible," she murmured sympathetically. "Were you abroad?"

"No. I was living in the village, working the fields along with the tenant farmers."

Her lips parted in shock. "I beg your pardon?"

James felt a similar sense of disbelief. He did not share his past with anyone, knowing the *ton's* propensity for gossip and cruel speculations into one's life. He cleared his throat. "You have shared a part of yourself with me, Lady Verity. You are trusting me with your secrets now, and for that reason…for that reason I too will share some of my past. Since I've never shared my history with anyone else, I will lay blame at your door if I hear this circulating among the masses."

Her eyes widened, and her fingers dug into the edges of the padded seat. "I do not gossip, my lord," she said softly. "I daresay you are not obliged to share."

James arched a brow and remained quiet.

She tapped her left foot several times, and shifted as if the seats were uncomfortable, then folded her arms across her middle. With a harrumph she said, "Oh, do continue!"

He laughed, impressed that her curiosity had held itself back for at least ten seconds. She glared at him with a perturbed furrow between her brows.

"My father neglected his duty, unable to rise to the occasion because he had been so lost in his grief," he said gruffly. "He loved my mother more than life itself, and I killed her."

Lady Verity stiffened but did not interrupt.

"I was a big, ugly brute who took her life during childbirth. My father never forgave me for that, so not only were the estates neglected, but so was I." James's earliest memories were of his father screaming to his nurse to take James from his sight. He'd been born too big. And as a brute he should work the fields. It had been unorthodox, shameful, but the old earl had forced his son to work the land alongside his tenant farmers. He'd denied him tutors, and the fine education the men of his line should have been given. He'd hidden him in the country along with his pain and his son's existence. Society knew there had been an heir, but they'd never met him. "I had no tutors or governesses. I was not sent to Eton or Oxford. I spent most of my life in the village of Cressingham. I was the ugly brute who took everything my father cherished, and he treated me like one."

Her eyes were red and it was evident to him she struggled with tears. James frowned, for he had not told her of any of the sufferings he had waded through—the vicious fights with the older boys, the pain of never knowing his mother, even how she looked, the hunger to hear a comforting word from his father always denied. "You are far too softhearted," he muttered.

She scowled at him. "I do not believe in speaking ill of the dead, but your father was an ass. My Aunt Jacintha died in childbirth several years ago, and her babe was exceedingly small. I believe it happens and it was terrible of him to blame you when he should have loved you endlessly because you were a part of her."

James smiled. "Thank you."

They stared at each other for several moments before she glanced away. He was curious about the blush reddening her cheeks and wondered what lingered within that mind of hers.

"You speak quite well for a man who grew up without formal education."

"My solace was found in books and from their pages my mind was edified. The village raised me. The servants raised me. I learned French from the village's dressmaker. They took their wages, pooled them together and bought me books and sweet treats. It was at their tables I enjoyed dinners and Christmas. It was at their homes I learned about family and love. So, when they needed me, I fought for them." And now his village and earldom were one of the most prosperous. Society would not bring him to shame for how he had attained his wealth.

A soft smile lit her face. "You are incredible, my lord. It must have been scary to be presented at court."

"I shook in my boots and bumbled in my speech," he said with a rueful smile. "But at the end, all was well."

The carriage slowed, and she shifted the small curtain by the windows. "We are in St. James," she said with a curious look his way.

"Yes."

"And we are slowing for the queue."

"Yes."

"Should we—"

"No."

An amused smile curved her generous lips. "You had no notion of my question."

"You wanted to know if we should descend and walk."

"Impressive," she said teasingly, before sobering.

"I want you to understand my rules before we enter. You are a lady, disguised as a young gent. Keep your head down. Do not speak unless absolutely necessary. And stay by my side at all times. If you must talk, deepen your voice, and speak low. To play the part you will also be required to nurse a drink. Whisky. Do not drink it. Simply… hold it, and sip occasionally. Is that understood, Lady Verity."

She nodded and he almost smiled at the shimmer of excitement in her golden eyes.

"Now take the time to compose yourself."

She tested that the short dark wig was firmly in place, tugged at her cravat, and even fiddled with her hat.

The carriage lurched ahead slowly, and he relaxed against the squabs. She licked her lips, and he wished by all that was holy he could disguise those too. They were so lush, carnal, and kissable.

Only a damn fool would think that wicked mouth belonged to a young man.

"I believe our first lesson should be on dancing," she said unexpectedly.

"If you think that is best."

A winsome smile curved her lips and drove the air from his lungs. "For God's sakes," he muttered, tugging at his cravat. "Under no circumstances must you smile tonight. *None*."

She made no reply to his request, but said, "Dancing is the first step in courtship. I believe it was understandable that Lady Susanna felt… slighted that you have never asked her to dance or observed any of the proper courtship rituals. Your proposal felt like a business transaction. So yes, we shall start with the elegant and beautiful art of dancing."

He nodded his agreement, thinking that maybe he had really approached courting of the lady in the wrong manner. Dancing, poetry, and flowers. Simple but clearly particularly important. And he thought about what they communicated and drew a blank. If every suitor asked for dances, recited poetry, and delivered flowers, how in God's name was any of it special?

Lady Verity cleared her throat. "Is Lady

Susanna the only lady you believed would make you a fine countess."

"She was the first lady to look at me," he said gruffly. The lady had flirted shamelessly with him at one of her father's political dinners. It had been an encouragement of sorts, except he had clearly ignored all the rules of courtship and had made an offer after a few more stilted meetings.

"What do you mean?"

"Most ladies of society look at me and see an animal."

Her golden eyes flashed with anger and he was entranced. "How absurd! I cannot credit you would believe such an odious notion."

"I've had married women, widows, reckless debutantes shamelessly make offers of the scandalous variety, yet at the balls pretend they do not know me. I've always been curious about the duality of their nature."

A hand fluttered to rest above her heart. "You've been with married women?"

How odd the disappointment in her voice stung and how damn glad he was that he'd lived by a code. "I normally booted those out."

She glanced away, but he saw the tiny smile at her lips before she suppressed it.

"It is time for us to enter. Let's go, Vincent."

She laughed. "Vincent. I like it."

Then they descended the carriage and made their way to the large bricked building, while James hoped he wasn't making a mistake taking such a fine lady into this den of sin and debauchery.

CHAPTER 6

Inside the Club was decadent. Verity's pulse skittered alarmingly and she hovered at the entrance almost scared to step into a place of sin and depravity. Fear and a dash of excitement coursed through her veins. Her breath trembled on her lips. The decor was one of luxury, red and green carpets covered the floor, and swaths of red and golden drapes twined themselves around massive white Corinthian columns. Dozens of tables were scattered in an organized sprawl on this lower floor, and many lords she recognized sat at tables playing faro, Macao, whist, and *vingt-et-un*.

Smoke wafted through the air from the many lit cigars, glasses clinked loudly as it appeared every gentleman had a drink in hand, and the clattering of dice echoed as they rolled on the tables. Verity swore she could hear the fine shuffling of the cards as they were flicked, cut, and shuffled with artistic expertise. Elegantly clad women with filigree masks on their faces, and a fortune in jewelry at their throats and ears reposed on chaise longues chatting and drinking champagne. This could have been a masquerade party held by a lady of the *ton*, or even one of the risqué parties the king was rumored to host, a nod to his wild and wicked days when he had been the Prince Regent. Yet, there was such an air of wickedness and conquest at this club that she doubted would ever exist at a society ball.

Atop the second-floor railing, stood a gentleman she recognized. Viscount Worsley, a man rumored to be dangerous and unpredictable. The man had a distinctively captivating presence, impeccably dressed in the first stare of fashion, and his dark blond hair shone like burnished gold under the thousands of candles hung suspended from magnificent chandeliers. He surveyed the crowd as if he were king, and the gambling lords and ladies his subjects. There was a rumor in the *ton* the viscount was part owner of a notorious club, but Verity hadn't paid any attention to it, for it did not concern her.

She glanced at James who seemed to be assessing her reception to his den of sin. It was as if he expected her to act missish and wail to be returned to her sanctuary. Somehow his air of expectancy inspired her to be spontaneous, naughty…*scandalous*. She sucked in a harsh breath and pushed away the ridiculous feelings. "So, this is how the sinful half live?" she asked archly.

The air crackled with the intensity of his stare, and she felt the ridiculous urge to remind him she was disguised as a lad. Another surely would not stare at a gentleman in such a disturbingly wicked manner. She glanced away briefly, and upon meeting his gaze, once again his expression was neutral. Had she imagined desire?

Or was it her unpardonable awareness she was foisting on the earl? He was truly irresistible, with those burning dark eyes and endearing smile, and a somewhat crooked nose.

"Follow me and keep close," he murmured.

They made their way through the tables toward the winding staircase. A few men stopped him, shook his hands, and even discussed James's support of a motion the Whig party wanted to argue in Parliament at its next session. Those who glanced at her overly long, received an introduction. James's cousin from the country, in town for a spot of gambling. She kept her head suitably low, her voice deep, and she was deemed as unimportant. They continued up the stairs where they passed Lord Worsley. Looking up as she approached, he quite openly studied her.

A smile curved his lips, and an arched brow was directed at James. Verity's heart tripped into an alarming beat.

"Worsley," James greeted coolly. "Has the match started?"

The viscount wrested his curious gaze from her. "About now. You made it in time. Will you challenge the winner? The purse is ten thousand pounds."

Verity almost expired from shock at the fortune named.

"Excellent. My cousin here, Vincent, is quite eager to witness one of your notorious prizefighting matches."

"Ah, Vincent is it?"

"Yes," James returned, and there was a throb of warning in his tone.

The viscount nodded, James continued on, and Verity followed, aware of the Viscount's stare on her back. "He recognized me," she said.

"No," James returned. "Not your identity. Simply that you are a lady."

"And is that cause for worry?"

"It is not. I would not risk your reputation in such a manner. Anonymity is respected and even expected once we enter these walls."

"I see." A little bit of her tension eased, as a man dressed in unrelenting black stood by a large oak door. He bowed slightly, then pushed open the massive door, and they stepped into another opulently fashioned room with soft dark green carpets cushioning their steps. The lights in this room were dimmer, the tables less raucous, and only a handful of ladies sat amongst the lords. And an expectant hush blanketed the room.

Smoke curled around the room, and footmen darted adroitly between the tables delivering drinks. James led her to a corner table which seemed more hidden amongst the shadows than most. Verity pulled out a chair and lowered herself, quite aware of James's presence as he sat in the chair next to her and stretched his long legs casually before him. It was as if everyone had waited for their presence, for a large roped area in the center of the prodigious room soon became the center of everyone's attention.

Two men approached the ropes, dipped under, and made way to the center of the ring. Her face heated to see the indecent manner in which they were dressed. Both men were stripped to the waist, their chests, and torsos on alarming display. A few of the women outrageously whistled. Every inch of her body felt on fire with embarrassment.

"The laws which govern pugilism are not observed here. In fact, prize matches like these are kept in remote areas on the outskirts of town with thousands of spectators," James said, his gaze on the men entering the ring. "We are not here to witness the sport of boxing."

And she understood. This was the art of fighting, the grittiness, the fear, and the thrill. "I understand."

A footman passed by their table and James snagged two glasses of amber liquid and handed her one.

"Remember—" he started to say.

"I know, nurse it, but keep a level head and do not drink."

The men wrapped thin leather strips that had been soaked in water or perhaps vinegar around their hands. It appeared little protection to her, and

Verity almost chuckled nervously as a man loudly announced their identities.

"Viscount Halifax and Marquess Durham."

Verity's soul froze, certain she heard the name Marquess Durham. She leaned forward. "These men are lords," she said faintly.

The earl threw her a surprised glance. "Only men of a certain caliber have a membership." He frowned. "You seem pale. Are you well?"

Hundreds of lanterns surrounding the ring were turned up, and there he was, the wretched marquess. A sick feeling of dread twisted through her and she battled it down. *I am with Lord Maschelly, I am safe.* It hovered on the tip of her tongue to tell him, but once again that shame and guilt which had always followed her refused to allow the words to spill. "I am well." Then she took a sip of the drink, coughing at the fiery burn which slid down her throat.

"Easy," the earl murmured, lightly touching her elbow.

A strange tingling jolt went up her arm and through her body, filling her with peculiar heat. It so alarmed her she snatched her hand away from him, almost knocking over the glass of whisky.

Lord Maschelly stiffened, and tilted his head

looking at her uncertainly. "I apologize, Lady Verity, it shall not happen again."

His piercing green eyes had become as flat and unreadable as a block of ice. He thought his touch had offended her when that was simply not the truth. She wanted to tell him so but felt he would not believe her words. Her flinch had been too visceral. Nor could she explain to him, his slight caress had caused her belly to flip and her heart to race.

The starting of the match prevented her from making a response, and she was absurdly grateful for it, sensing she would have done or said something silly and reckless. The fight was rough, and from where she sat, several feet away, she could hear the slaps and thuds as fists met flesh. With each sound she flinched, and she had to steel herself against the instinctive reaction and forced herself to observe the match.

The viscount kicked at Durham's knees, but the man danced with surprising grace and dexterity out of the way.

Lord Maschelly chuckled as if he admired the display of skill, and Verity felt ill. *Courage, Verity, going forward, courage*.

"Such a move would be illegal if this had been a

boxing match," he explained. "There would be no kicking or hitting below the waist. But not in here. And a fight in real life is very much the same, my lady. No rules. Only what is necessary to win."

No rules.

The lesson the earl wanted to hammer home resounded with each brutal punch. A sense of helpless fury surged through her, for Verity realized the dreaded marquess was a skilled fighter, and if he were to ever attack her again, how could she escape him? Not that she ever intended to be alone with the vile snake again.

At one moment she shifted, and found the earl watching her with a keenly observant eye. She looked away from him and took another healthy swallow of the whisky.

The match seemed to take forever, when in actuality only a few minutes passed. It was all so barbaric and improper. In quick form, the marquess knocked the viscount flat on his back, and the crowd cheered raucously.

"Another match will be coming soon. Do you wish to watch it?" the earl asked.

"No," she said quickly. "I believe I understand your lesson."

He nodded and stood, and Verity followed suit.

Ice congealed in her veins when she saw the marquess, more appropriately attired, headed toward them.

"James?" she was so alarmed she called the earl by his name.

His eyes sharpened, studying her with curious intensity. "What is it?"

She swallowed, hating the awful feelings stirring in her stomach, and then both the marquess and the viscount were there.

"Maschelly," the marquess said jovially. "Just the man I wanted to see. I've always wanted a match with one of the bare-knuckle kings. What do you say we arrange—"

Unable to bear hearing the voice which had haunted her dreams for so long, she skirted from around the table, and with hurried steps made her way to the door.

"Vincent?" Lord Maschelly's tone was sharp, questioning, concerned, but she did not slow.

"Who is the pup?" she heard the marquess ask and she almost cast up her accounts.

Verity broke into a run, passed many startled patrons, and down the stairs. She collided into a footman, and the tray of drinks tipped to the floor with a resounding crash.

She tried to dart around the mess, and someone grabbed her. The shock of it pulled a startled scream from her. The hand disappeared, and before she could process what had happened, the man sailed in the air and crashed against a wall with a pained groan.

"No one touches him," Lord Maschelly commanded, his tone flat and lethal.

Many gazes landed on her, then to the man behind her, but she did not pause, rushing outside as if the devil chased her.

Once there, she took deep breaths of fresh air, hating the tears pricking her eyes. Her throat burned, anger and shame filled her heart, and she stuffed a fist in her mouth choking on a ragged sob.

"Verity," a soft voice said. "I should have never brought you here. I was a damn idiot."

She spun around. "James…I…I mean Lord Maschelly…" Words deserted her as she stared at him. He seemed fierce and ruthless, as if he had arrived to vanquish whomever or whatever had upset her. He stepped toward her and she jerked back. It was an instinctive movement and she felt wretched for the shuttered look which covered his expression.

"I am not afraid of you," she burst out

passionately. "You…you are the very first gentleman I have felt safe around in years. I cannot explain it because you are so very large and intimidating…but I just *do*…because you are so real and unpretentious."

※

JAMES'S MUSCLES were knotted with a terrible tension. He moved slowly, heavily, toward her as if drawn by a magnet. He saw her struggle to remain still and not jerk from him and it shredded something deep inside of his heart. Who had abused such sweet gentleness and created the wary mistrust staring at him with such large wounded eyes? What had frightened her?

"It was wrong of me to take you here," he said gruffly, his heart throbbing with guilt…and fear that something might have scared her because he had pushed too soon. His rage had festered like a wound when someone had dared touched her.

"No, thank you. I needed to understand."

"Do not thank me when I could have gotten you hurt, badly."

"Do not be melodramatic," she chided. "The man barely touched me." She wanted to sound brave and nonchalant, but her eyes shimmered with unshed tears.

"May I come closer?"

She lowered her eyes away from his steady gaze. "Yes."

"What made you run?"

A sob hitched in her throat and an icy resolve filled him. Whatever or whoever had hurt her would be vanquished. It was a risk, touching her, but he needed to see her face. James placed a finger beneath her chin gently and urged her face upward.

She reacted, gripping his finger, but she did not push him away. Instead, she clutched at his finger as if it were a lifeline. Her touch against his knuckles was like the delicate brush of the wings of a butterfly.

Large wounded eyes peered up at him. "Sometimes I hear his laugh in my dreams, deafening and suffocating me."

And he knew in that moment he would kill the man who had put such shadows in her eyes and pain in her voice.

"Tell me his name."

She closed her eyes briefly before snapping them open. "I…"

He raked his fingers through his hair, turning its

careful disarray into a tangled mess. "He was inside just now. That is why you ran outside. It was unbearable seeing him again."

Her throat worked on a swallow. "Yes."

"Tell me his name," he repeated.

"Why?"

"So I may call him out and put a bullet through his black soul."

"Do not be foolish! Dueling is illegal!"

"Verity—"

She stepped away from him and he felt bereft at the loss of her touch. "No, and if you shall say such madness, I'll never reveal who he is to you!"

"I'll not get caught," he said on an irritated grunt.

"I'll not risk you," she cried, thumping his chest.

Something at once primal and tender shifted inside of him. "Why, Verity?"

The air tightened with an unexpected tension. Her lashes swept down across her cheekbones, hiding her expression from him.

"Look at me," he said gruffly.

"I do not know. Just know that I'll not risk your life or reputation over that snake."

"And are you not doing the same now, wanting to fight, to learn about the uglier side of life?"

Her face was pale but proud. "I need to do this…at any cost, but I am not selfish enough to risk another's life because of my pains," she said hoarsely.

She looked so young and vulnerable, he wanted to drag her into the cage of his arms and promise he would slay her fears. Lady Verity pressed a hand to her mouth, shaking her head when he would have moved to touch her.

He lowered his hand and was about to move away when she stepped closer. There was both delicacy and strength in the face that peered up at him. *Meet me halfway*, her eyes seemed to beseech him, and sensing he would regret giving into the temptation, James reached out and took her hands within his.

CHAPTER 7

Verity froze. A man was touching her. And not just any man—James, the earl of Maschelly. For so long she had avoided having any gentleman too close to her, even dancing had become uncomfortable, but she had tolerated it to the best of her abilities. She waited for that awful feeling to cramp her stomach, and for the sweat to coat her skin, even though it was such a simple touch, palm to palm, and they both wore evening gloves. None of the usual reaction came, and unaccountably Verity wished they had been skin to skin. Even with the gloves separating a more intimate touch she felt the heat of him, and something even more bewildering, simply because she had not felt so in years—comfort, warmth, protected.

"I can see that I've shocked you," he murmured.

No, my yearning to feel your skin upon mine did. She licked her lips and the eyes which had followed the moment darkened with undefinable emotions.

The earl guided her away from the entrance of the club, and toward the line of parked carriages. Instead of heading for his coach, he tugged her to the side of the building, encasing them in partial shadows. The glow of the gas lamp and the hovering fog shed only a small amount of light, but it was as if his glittering eyes were a beacon onto themselves. Truly, Verity had never seen eyes so wickedly splendid.

"Did you not realize we would be required to touch? When we fight…when you teach me to dance?" he murmured gently.

No…she hadn't thought that far ahead, and she felt ridiculous. "I…"

"Do you fear me touching you?"

Yes…no…. Everything about him was large, and she was all too aware of the breadth of his shoulders, his height, and his large hands. This man could crush her so easily. Even more so than the marquess, because Lord Maschelly was unquestionably more virile, powerful, and dangerous.

"I would *never* hurt you," he said gruffly. "Never, my lady. I swear it on my honor."

Verity closed her eyes and inhaled deeply. She was suddenly acutely conscious of scents and noises drifting to her through the night—the murkiness of the Thames, rotting fruits, but something fresh and clean beneath it all, the warm male fragrance of the man himself. A few carriages rumbled by, yet neither moved. His hand fell away from hers, and upon opening her eyes, she watched in dazed bemusement as he tugged off his gloves and stuffed them in his pockets.

Her heart raced uncontrollably like a runaway carriage. Then he placed two of his warm fingers beneath her chin and nudged. Clearly, he wanted her to meet his eyes once more, and she was afraid to, for Verity felt as if she was falling into something she did not understand. Nothing felt familiar, nothing felt safe. No…the earl felt safe.

A fierce, painful longing surged through her, and oddly the need was to step into his arms. A quiver of uncertainty went through Verity. Why did she feel so with him? A man like the earl was not for her. Even before her attack, she'd had it all planned

—the type of fair gentleman she would marry, where they would honeymoon, the kind of wondrous fun they would have. The earl did not fit that old musing, but she felt helpless to stop the curious hunger awakening in her heart.

The tip of her chin tingled. Her skin seemed to burn beneath his fingers, yet she didn't want to move.

"Are you afraid of me, Lady Verity?" he asked again, and she suspected the answer was of immense importance to him. How fascinating that his awkward touch could be both rough and infinitely gentle. The calluses Lady Susanna had cried prettily about were comforting, real.

The weird sensation jerking in her belly did not feel like fear, but she could not identify it for she had never felt anything like this before.

"I am not afraid of you," she whispered.

A look of wonder, possibly admiration settled on his face, before smoothing into a bland mask. "Good," he said and lowered his arm. "Let's get you home."

Her thoughts muddled for a few moments. "Are we not starting our lessons tonight?"

"It is late. Almost eleven. And you have learned enough today. I will take you home now." There was an undercurrent in his tone she was unable to decipher.

"In these clothes?"

"My home first, then off you go. I will send my coach for you on Thursday. Never come to me without your veil."

She nodded and they made their way to the parked carriage in silence. They sat on opposite seats and the carriage lantern burned low, creating a too intimate atmosphere. Yet neither made the effort to introduce conversation as the coach pulled away. His brief smile hinted at a discomfort. A heart-pounding awareness burned through her. Then a shocking surge of heat quivered through her and Verity desperately tried to force her silly heart to beat to its normal rhythm. She leaned back against the squabs, that single truth rattling her—Lord Maschelly was unsettled by her, *liked* her perhaps, and he had wisely retreated.

And I must do the same.

Yet at this moment she could not recall precisely why a man like the earl was unsuitable for a lady like her. Verity fiercely reminded herself that their connection was for only one purpose—learn enough so that when she closed her eyes, she wouldn't ever see the face of her nightmare. That was the only reason she had aligned with a man like Lord Maschelly. And she needed to remember it always lest she deceive her heart to pain.

❦

Dear Aunt Imogen,

I do hope my letter finds you in splendid health. I am trying to enjoy the season as you commanded. Last week I went to the theater and had a few outings in Hyde Park with Lady Caroline and the Duchess Carlyle. They are the best of ladies and we have become dear friends. The weather has been pleasant, and I am sorry to hear of the constant rains in Bedfordshire. I know you love and miss your gardens and I promise you shall be tending them soon. Mamma is well, and she received your last letter with pleasure. Arthur is the same boorish man that you'd last seen. He has decreed that I marry one Lord Aldridge, but I am adamant to forge my own path. I want what you had, Aunt Imogen, a rare and beautiful love with a man of my choosing. I promise to visit in a few weeks when I tire of the frivolities of the season.

Your loving niece, Verity.

WHEN THE EARL WAS WICKED

VERITY CAREFULLY FOLDED the single sheet of paper and added a wafer. She happily wrote to her aunt weekly, for her aunt had vowed never to return to the foul London air which she blamed for her prolonged illness. The doctors had diagnosed melancholia and overwrought nerves, but Verity believed it had been a broken heart which had ailed Aunt Imogen who had lost her husband a few years before. They hadn't been blessed with any children in their five and twenty years of marriage, and she hadn't been the same since his passing.

Aunt Imogen had been the only person who had believed Verity when she had named the marquess a debauched snake. She had been the one to come upon them in the grotto with the marquess's heavy weight pinning Verity to the damp earth. Aunt Imogen thought she had interrupted a lover's tryst, until she had seen the state of Verity's clothing and her bruised cheeks. It still amazed Verity that even with her aunt's unflinching support, her mother and brother had been so quick to turn a blind eye. The sisters' close relationship had been altered to mamma's distress, but Aunt Imogen was not forgiving of their disloyalty.

A knock sounded and she glanced up as her

lady's maid entered. "Her ladyship bids you to attend her in the drawing room, Lady Verity."

"I shall be along shortly," she said with a small smile which felt tight.

Her toilette had already been completed for the morning, her hair coiffed in a simple but elegant chignon, and she had donned a simple but graceful long-sleeved dark blue day dress with a scalloped neckline. She did not anticipate spending the day in the presence of her mother. She had escaped it yesterday by calling on Pippa for the better part of that afternoon, and then dining with the Duchess and her wonderful husband. Of course, mamma had been happy to let her go, admiring the well-connected company Verity kept.

The only thing she anticipated today was the earl's carriage arriving for her under the banner of secrecy. She was eager to start learning the rudiments of fighting. Even though a part of her suspected she might need more than fighting lessons to overcome the fear seeing the marquess always inspired. When he had approached James at the club, she should have been stronger, but how her heart had pounded, and the memories had ravaged her.

There had been a sick sense of fear that he

might have recognized her and acted in a dastardly fashion. James wouldn't have allowed it. Verity smiled. How odd that she should have such faith in a man she hardly knew. And what was it about him which made her find his presence relaxing? She recalled the harsh upbringing he'd endured and her admiration for him rose like a gentle swell.

Sounds of servants' feet in the hallway urged her to stand. Her mother would not be pleased to be kept waiting. With an impatient sigh, Verity made her way from the chamber to the ground floor and rested the letter on the mantle in the hallway. The butler would frank and post it along with the others on the silver salver. Verity then made her way to the drawing room, foregoing the breakfast room.

Her mother awaited her, the room artfully arranged with flowers and a tea service.

"You've overslept," her mother said, her lips thin with disapproval. "I am sure you are aware we are to receive several callers today. It is almost noon, Verity."

"I wrote to Aunt Imogen and lost track of the time."

Her mother's face softened at the mention of her sister, and Verity did not like to admire her delicate beauty, not when she believed her mother's heart was blackened by selfish desires and greed. Countess Sutcliffe was a lady in her early forties, and beautiful with lustrous dark hair which showed no gray. In truth her features held a unique blush of youth, her light blue eyes still sparkled with vitality. There had been a time when Verity had loved her and sought to emulate her grace and elegance.

Now, she was not sure what she felt for her mother. There was always a wash of pain and disappointment whenever she saw her. And it gutted her that she wondered some days if she loved her mother still. Or if her mother loved her.

"Lord Aldridge and his mother are to call today. I trust you will make a good impression."

"There is a rumor that Lord Aldridge is impoverished," Verity said, sitting, shifting on the plush sofa to face her mother. "It seems my inheritance of twenty thousand pounds from papa and my dowry of another ten thousand is quite appealing. I know talk of money is crass mamma, but surely someone should tell the viscount that papa made his will so that my inheritance is my own and does not become my husband's upon marriage. Perhaps then he would be less evident in a pursuit I am not interested in."

Her mother's eyes flashed. "Upon my word, you will mind your tongue, Verity! It is these willful ways of yours that led to...."

Her mother looked away and Verity stared at her in pained silence.

"It is my willful tongue which allowed a dishonest libertine to try and take my virtue?" Though she was just as surprised her mother had been about to mention the incident. Neither mamma nor Albert normally spoke of the pain of Verity's past of their own volition.

Red swept along her mother's elegant cheekbones and Verity fought down the guilt which had tormented her in the early days. If she had not flirted with the marquess, allowed his chaste kisses, walked alone with him by the lake and the grotto... she would have been safe. It had taken her a long time to realize that the dishonor belonged to him alone, and it had been the gentle guidance of her dear Aunt Imogen which had helped Verity.

When her mamma finally shifted her eyes back to Verity there was such heartbreak and pain in them, it almost strangled her. "Mamma?"

Her mother's eyes welled with tears and Verity's hand fluttered to her throat.

"Verity, my dear—"

A knock interrupted, and the butler entered to announce Lady Metcalf and her two daughters. Verity stood to receive their callers and her hands trembled as she smoothed down the skirts of her dress. There had been such strong emotions on her mother's face, it reminded Verity of a time when her mother had kissed her bruises and hugged her before putting her to bed.

Lady Metcalf and her daughters entered, and her mother shifted into the consummate hostess, greeting them with pleasant warmth, and ringing for more tea and pastries. Verity hardly paid attention to the ladies of the *ton* who made their weekly calls at their townhouse—a few matrons her mother's age with their marriageable daughters in obedient tow, all with the aim of securing her brother as a suitor. Before two in the afternoon they had received four callers. One was Lord Aldridge with whom Verity was obliged to take a turn in the small gardens at the back of the townhouse in full view of her mother from the drawing room.

He was a very elegant young gentleman who boasted a fashionable appearance. He was slimly built, with plain features, but with an air of considerable self-consequence. Which would be expected by some since he was a viscount with a rumored income of over thirty thousand pounds a year. Could he truly be impoverished as the rumors hinted and sought an heiress?

He was surprisingly pleasant and amusing, but Verity only felt a sense of wariness around him and could not escape the knowledge that he and the marquess Durham were close friends. Did pits of snakes not writhe together? They spent several minutes in discourse with an exchange of very proper nothings—the weather, the latest *on dits*, and even a lemon pie he had eaten earlier.

"Oh dear!" she said in a deliberately dramatic fashion, but with charming civility. "I just recalled I have an urgent meeting, Lord Aldridge. I must take my leave right away. Please apologize to your mother for me."

"Certainly," he replied with such cordiality she felt a slight pang of guilt for her dismissive attitude. "I do hope everything is well, Lady Verity."

"My lord," Verity said, "May I speak frankly?"

He dealt her a considering glance. "It would please me."

"I will not consent to a courtship if that is your desire. I am certain my brother made some assurance that I will agree to such a union, but he misspoke. I apologize sincerely."

Lord Aldridge's eyes widened and a flush ran along his neckline. Then he assessed her in narrowed-eye contemplation. "You are a delicately nurtured female with little understanding of the world, Lady Verity. Your brother and I believe we shall suit very well indeed," he said chidingly, as if she were a simpleton.

Verity lifted a brow. "You are affable and gentlemanly, but I will only be persuaded to marry a man I have the deepest affections for. And one who loves me in return. I suspect that will not be the situation with you."

"You are very decided with your arguments," he replied testily.

"It would be silly to be hesitant on matters of such grave importance. We will not suit, and I shall not be persuaded against my heart…*ever*. I also suspect my brother neglected to mention my inheritance is not transferable upon marriage. And with the rumors swirling of your gambling debt, my dowry is not a tempting enough morsel to justify persuasion on your part, my lord."

Lord Aldridge's face mottled with the force of his anger, but she lifted her chin and held her ground. He turned on his heel and walked off, his lips tightly compressed. Her mamma would be furious but Verity could hardly drum up the withal to care. She went inside and collected her pelisse, hat, reticule, and an umbrella. The sky appeared decidedly overcast, quite befitting her current mood.

As she exited the townhouse, she could hear mamma's twinkling laughter as she entertained her callers. Fortunately, Lady Caroline also lived in Grosvenor Square, only a few minutes' walk from Verity's own home. Walking briskly, she arrived at Caroline's home just as she was being handed up in a carriage by a livered footman. A lady's maid, who was to act as a chaperone, hovered by the carriage steps.

"Verity darling, how good of you to come," Caroline cried, her pretty gray eyes sparkling with her usual humor and delight, her dark red ringlets styled fashionably to set off her gentle beauty. "I'm off to High Holborn for a spot of shopping, would you care to accompany me?"

Verity made her way over and was also assisted into the equipage by the footman. "I would be delighted, Caro. Though I am perturbed by the frequency of your shopping. It was only last week we bought an indecent number of hats and no less than three new parasols."

"I only indulge every Monday and Thursday," Caroline objected with a wink. "Papa can afford it and I do like new dresses."

They laughed, and as the carriage rumbled off, Verity informed her of all that had happened since they last spoke.

"Oh Dear! Lord Maschelly took *you* to a gambling club and a prizefighting match? That man is truly wicked!"

Once they arrived in High Holborn, they strolled arm in arm, the footman keeping abreast at a suitable distance. They made several purchases, pored over fashion plates, and ordered a few gowns. They ran into Miss Cecelia Markham, a pleasant young lady with whom she was well-acquainted from Bedfordshire. They all visited Gunter's together and indulged in an ice, chatting and laughing over the latest *on dits*, before promising to call on each other next week.

Upon returning home, her mother waited, fairly vibrating with anger. She was somewhat mollified by the shopping boxes, for such actions signaled to her that Verity was fully on board with the plan to net a wealthy lord, preferably of her and Albert's choosing. Refusing to quarrel with her mother, she hurried to her room, and closed the door with a *snick*.

Those diversions had kept her mind occupied for the day, but now Verity fairly vibrated with nerves and excitement to be on her way to meet with Lord Maschelly. Three hours remained before his carriage and coachman would arrive behind the mews.

After indulging in a lengthy bath, Verity attempted to read the riveting serial *The Tower of London* by William Ainsworth, but it provided little distraction against the trepidation and excitement dominating her thoughts. At six thirty, the dinner gong rang. Supper with her brother and mother was its usual torturous affair, but she bore it, and retired early pleading another headache. Though her mother had gone to her literary society meeting, and her brother to one of his clubs, she was careful in dressing in a simple and serviceable dark bombazine gown. Verity slipped the veil and hat over her tightly pinned chignon and made her way outside to the back of the mews. Once again, the nondescript coach waited, and she lingered for a few minutes watching the surroundings before she hurried over to the equipage.

As she approached, the coachman hopped

down from his seat, and knocked down the carriage steps. After entering and settling against the squabs, her thoughts drifted to the upcoming lesson, and she tried to convince herself the heady anticipation flowing through her veins and tumbling low in her belly had nothing to do with actually seeing the earl.

Nothing at all.

CHAPTER 8

Almost an hour after their lesson had started, Verity took a break. Dressing in breeches and a flowing linen shirt had allowed her much freedom of movement and flexibility as Lord Maschelly had shown her how to make a proper fist, and then how to throw it. Those motions had been repeated several times until she was confident, she could actually plant a facer on someone if it was warranted.

She had declared it, and the man had winked at her.

"It is time to resume," he said, prowling towards her once more in that graceful masculine way of his.

She swallowed the last of the water and set the

glass on the table beside the carafe. Verity met him in the center of the room.

"Remember my aim is to teach you to defend… to escape," he said, watching her keenly.

She nodded, uncertainly.

"Everything before had been about making a fist, the poise and elegant footwork of boxing. Knowing those moves will build up your agility and confidence. Each session we will practice until those moves become an extension of yourself. You are a very quick learner, one of the quickest I've ever seen, I assure you in no time you will be proficient."

Warmth burst inside her chest like sunshine itself, and she grinned. "I do believe I am," she drawled, shuffling her feet in the manner he had shown her.

He laughed, the sound a low rumble of delight which stole her breath. "You should laugh more," she said.

"I shall when I am given a reason." He said this with a smile, and an almost tender expression in his eyes. "I want you to learn about escape. Do I have your permission to touch you?"

She licked her lips, an unexplained nervous tension thrumming through her. "Yes."

"I do not refer to a fleeting touch."

"I understand," she replied huskily.

"Good."

Then he moved with swiftness and grabbed her from behind. A loud roaring sounded in her ears and she panted furiously.

"Relax," he murmured, his tone gentle and soothing as if he spoke to a skittish horse. "It is only me. That panic you are feeling now…that helplessness, breathe through it, and take control of the situation. You can drop your weight. The surprise of it will break my grip."

She complied and they tumbled. They repeated the exercise with him showing her various ways to escape his unrelenting clutch. With each success her confidence grew, and somehow, so did the anger inside of her. At one point when he held her down, the sense of powerlessness had been so great she had screamed her rage and frustration. And had gone for his eyes, a very vulnerable spot as he had taught her.

He had recoiled from her with agile speed and grace and grinned at her proudly. "As I said, very quick pupil."

"My lord! I could have hurt you," she cried, considerably distressed.

"I do believe it is time you called me James, especially after almost plucking my eyes out."

Verity gasped and the man laughed. "Very well...James."

His eyes darkened. "Thank you, Verity."

They had another brief period of rest. She drank more water, nibbled on a delicious sandwich, and then they were back at sparring. Several moments later, she rolled away from him and scrambled to her knees. Every muscle in her body was sore; she could manage only a pained shuffle. "We have been training for over two hours," she panted.

"Your endurance needs improvement. Giving up?" he drawled.

Verity grinned, amazed she could feel so sore yet gloriously alive. "*Never.*"

At least another hour passed in a blur of learning where to hit, punching, kicking, resting in between, and eating oranges. Now they lay on the floor, and she felt worn. "I never knew boxing involved learning about kicking a man...a man... you know *where*," she muttered, horrified to realized she still blushed at that bit of knowledge.

"I am not teaching you boxing."

She turned her head to where he too lay a few

feet from her. He stared at the ceiling, and she studied his left profile. The man was astonishingly handsome.

"You are teaching me how to fight," she murmured.

"Yes. And fighting is unfair, gritty, raw, and violent."

Something unspoken lingered in the room, and she felt uneasy. "You do not think I am capable of…of fighting if required. I am too *ladylike* and gentle," she said, with a reproving glance at the earl.

Yet Verity acknowledged it was a deep fear in her heart. What if all this risk was for naught. What if she never used the skills she learned and worse… what if she was called upon to use them and could not. The shame of it would kill her.

"While you are an apt pupil, you are very delicate."

"I am stronger than I appear," she snapped.

"Perhaps. If your brother will not defend your dignity when needed, a husband would."

"A marriage will be announced soon."

He jerked as if he'd been slapped.

"You are engaged?"

"No, but I am aware of the man whom I wish

to marry. Well not the man himself but of his attributes and qualities."

The corner of the earl's mouth curled upward. "And what merits are pleasing to Lady Verity?" His smile was the most irresistible she had ever seen, and his tone was like dark velvet.

She blushed and looked away.

"Come now, your fierceness has been incurable so far, do not attempt shyness now."

She scowled at him, and the dratted man smiled. "I do not mock the sincerity of your desire, I am only curious about you."

There was that warm glow inside again.

"My ideal husband is fair and very elegant. We are of a similar height, and he is slim in built. The *ton* should respect him, but he does not need to be overly popular. He is kind, humorous, smart, and attentive. We should be quite close in age so that we grow old together with little chance of one dying long before the other. He should bring me flowers often, sing with me for I so love singing."

"Good God," he muttered. "I cannot credit ladies have such stipulations. I think it is impossible to dictate who the heart should fall in love with."

Love. Such a tender sentiment from the earl startled her. "And I suppose *you* believe in love?"

"Of course, why would I not?"

She had no reply to that arched question. "I do declare men have expectations as well. Most in society wish for a wife of fortune, and to have little interest beyond serving their husband and household."

"I have no such ridiculous expectations," he uttered darkly.

She smiled triumphantly. "But you have others! Do you not wish to marry a woman of quality? One whose father has political influence? You have yet to make your mark in parliament and your ambitions lean in that direction. The rumors say so."

"I suppose that means it *must* be true?"

"True enough. Both ladies and gentlemen have an expectation in their heart as to what they want in their partners. They are simply different," she said with a touch of hauteur.

He grunted, as if annoyed. "And what will your husband who sounds to me like one of those elegant and proper dandies think of you knowing to fight, and how you came by the knowledge?"

She bit back a laugh. "He will not know unless necessary."

"Ah…a marriage with deception then, so a normal *ton* marriage from what I have observed."

Verity smothered an exclamation of annoyance. "You are trying to vex me!"

"Perhaps," he said with provoking amusement. "And I do not need a wife with connections. While it would be beneficial to my future ambitions, it is not a requirement. I can make it anywhere, no matter how brutal the climb, on my own terms."

There was that unbending resolve in his tone, and she realized it was his innate pride which had pushed him to be the man that he is today. Many would have crumbled under the expectations of turning around the fortunes of several estates and to provide for so many dependents. Most would have married a woman of fortune and not done much more.

But not James.

"I would like my countess to possess intelligence, kindness, and all the social graces and proper knowledge of how to behave in society to help our children take their place in the world. In that regard I am sorely lacking, with blunt edges that will never be smooth enough for me to wade through these shark-infested high society waters without a few bites. Though I promise I will bite back."

Yet he sounded so uncaring. And a pulse of awareness echoed inside of her. "But most of all, you wish for a lady who would accept you how you are. That is one of the reasons you are no longer interested in pursuing Lady Susanna."

He stared at her for a moment, and then said, "Your break is over."

With startling speed, he rolled atop her, caught her wrists, and caged them at her side, rendering her helpless. A wave of heat burst through Verity, like molten lava.

He dipped his face perilously close to hers, their noses almost touching. "Use all resources I've shown you so far to escape."

She struggled to push his massive weight from her body.

"Remember, Verity. Bite. Knee in the groin. Scream if need be. One aspect of fighting is learning how to be scrappy. You are small, but quick and agile. That quickness is your greatest advantage."

She lifted her hips with a hard jerk, but his grip did not break. The man did not even budge. And most mortifying, she had to stop as a ripple of heat shuddered through her. How humiliating that he was not similarly affected. She did everything to mask how unsettled his presence atop her body made her feel. It was not fear, nor a sense of disgust or worry that he would hurt her. James was being a gentleman in every way. It was her secretly hoping he would kiss her. Verity felt awful. She wriggled and bucked beneath him, wicked thoughts stirring despite every attempt to bury them deep in her mind.

"Think," he snapped, sounding rough and tight. "Escape me!"

A snarl of frustration slipped from her, and she reared up and brushed her lips along his collarbone. When he did not release her, she pressed her lips to his.

James froze in astonished silence, then lurched from her so quickly, he knocked his elbows onto the floor. He winced and scrabbled to his feet, and she awkwardly stood.

"I am terribly mortified, James. I cannot imagine why I did that. I am so sorry!" Verity wanted to die from the humiliation coursing through her. She had *kissed* him. It had been a quick peck on the lips, and it had wrought the loosening of arms she'd needed for a quick escape.

She pressed a finger to her lips. "I was not thinking, James!"

The look on his face made her want to disappear. What had she been thinking? But that was the problem wasn't it? Often she did not think, acting on sheer impulse.

"Think nothing of it," he said gruffly walking a few paces from her. "The element of surprise is always good. You caught me off guard and you escaped. Well done." He glanced around. "This session is over. Good night, Lady Verity."

Then he walked away, leaving her standing there like a fool. Dear God, surely, he would terminate their agreement. Why had she been so foolish and impulsive? And now there would be a terrible, awful tension between them if he would ever agree to another session.

Verity wasn't certain how long she stood there before darting through the door, and down the hallway. At the base of the stairs she glanced up to see him just reaching the landing to the second floor. She hurried after him, panting slightly, ignoring the aching in her muscles. A door closed in the distance and she made her way to it, lifting her hand to knock.

It was highly improper, her conscience warned her. Surely this was his bedchamber. But she had to talk to him. The manner in which he had dismissed her did not bode well, and she had to convince him it was an aberration, and it would *never* happen again. And certainly, standing in the doorway of a man's chamber and talking to him, could not be more indecent and scandalous than that man teaching her to fight!

Verity knocked on the door and waited. When no answer came, she knocked again. After a few more moments, impatience and anxiety had her testing the door. It eased open under her palm, and she faltered into remarkable stillness.

Her chest went so tight, she could scarcely breathe. James was naked!

His thighs and calves were thick and powerful, stomach and buttocks lean and delineated with muscle. *I am staring at a naked man.* Her heart thrummed painfully hard and her entire body tingled. Dear heaven, she had never felt like this before.

She must have made a sound, for he glanced around, and their gazes collided. It was the earl's turn to freeze and it was as if he turned into a marble. A multitude of emotions flickered over his face before it became impassive. Yet he made no move to grab for a banyan or his clothes. The doorknob slipped from her nerveless fingers, and

Verity turned and ran as if rabid dogs chased her. Her response had been too strong, too frightening, and she wanted only to hide away.

She dashed into the room assigned to her, made her way behind the screen, and started to remove the small shirt and trousers with trembling hands. Verity paused and rang the bell for Grace. Oh God, what had she been thinking to follow him? The maid arrived and a few minutes later Verity was once more garbed in her chemise, pantaloons, petticoats, and her dark green gown. Her hair was fixed and her small dark hat and veil once more covered her features.

She fought for a sense of calm, hating how heated her cheeks and entire body felt. What must he think of her? And why had he not followed her? Why had he not berated her for the kiss? Verity wasn't certain she wanted the answer to those questions, but she could not leave without an apology. Her sleep would be haunted. And she absolutely must know if they were to continue with lessons.

She made her way downstairs, and paused at the base of the stairs, gripping the carved mahogany railing. This time she would await an answer before daring to open his door. In fact, she would wait for him to come to her. Perhaps in the drawing room.

"His lordship is in the library," a bland voice said from behind her.

She turned. "Thank you, Fenton," she said to the butler with a nod, then sauntered toward the library. Once there she knocked.

"Come."

She opened the door and slipped inside. "I apologize, my lord. I was not thinking, and I ask you not to be upset—"

He turned around with such fierceness, she stumbled back. But it wasn't fear that filled her. Verity's belly went hot and her knees weak at the expression of raw desire on his face. *He wants me.* A hand fluttered to her mouth as she stared at him with ill-concealed shock. Breathing was nearly impossible as she waited for him to move, to say something, for she was robbed of further speech. He was singularly inappropriate to be a romantic interest. He was too big…too vital, too dominant. So why did she feel so breathless…so achy with unfathomable need?

Finally, he said, "I believed you had left, Lady Verity. I thought the sight of my nudity would have chased you all the way to Grosvenor Square and beset your nerves for the rest of the week."

The room suddenly seemed to be without air.

"I…no, I had to change first," she said inanely.

"Of course, how remiss of me."

They stood there, holding each other's gaze, and the tension in the air felt fraught with such peril she trembled.

His eyes sharpened. "Are you afraid?"

It took her a moment to answer. "Of you?"

His regard was too steady to be comfortable. "Yes."

"Of course not, my lord."

He glanced away briefly, but she'd spied the stark flash of relief in his beautiful eyes. His regard settled on her once more. "You'll always be safe with me. I apologize if I scared you earlier when I held you down. It was ungentlemanly of me knowing of your past. I will endeavor to ask permission whenever I wish to impart such lessons."

Something cold melted inside of Verity. "Thank you, but an apology is unnecessary. I was not afraid. Not once. And I am heartened to know our lessons will continue," she said softly, fighting the ridiculous need to walk into his arms.

She did it anyway, and hugged him, ignoring his

soft grunt of surprise. There was no logical explanation for why she did it. It was improper, and intimate. Yet she hugged him fiercely, distantly aware of the fine trembling in her frame.

Thump. Thump. Thump. How fast his heart beat, and Verity knew it was for her. She withdrew from his arms and glanced up at him. She was venturing into unknown territory. Verity should be scared, but she was enthralled.

She lifted his hand to her lips and kissed his palm. *Stop!* Deep down, a frightened part of her cried, but she did not obey. James closed his eyes briefly, as if he hoarded the feel of her lips on his skin. He hauled her up to him, and when she gasped, he took her mouth with his. James brushed the lightest of kisses across her mouth before capturing her lower lip between his teeth to bite down gently, teasing her lips to part with soft nibbles and hot, urgent kisses.

Soft whimpering noises escaped from deep in her throat, and she was helpless to stop. Verity had never felt more gloriously, joyously alive in all her life.

CHAPTER 9

James felt a deep conviction that he would regret yielding to the temptation of the woman in his arms. But she'd lifted her sweet face to his and he became lost. He stumbled with her to the chaise longue by the fire, and twisted so she landed atop his chest, never once releasing her mouth from his. Verity's moan slipped from her mouth to his, the sound so soft…surprised yet wanton, James felt he finally understood the true meaning of hunger. It flamed through him like a fiery whip of desire, and he kissed her over and over, unable to recall her innocence in the face of such enticing carnality.

One kiss from her would never be enough, and he had known a man with his brutish and inelegant ways would never have suited a fine lady of quality as herself. Earl or no, she wanted a certain refinement and he did not possess that, and never would, even with a thousand lessons. Even now, a brutal ache pounded through his cock, demanding he ravish her with the hottest of pleasures.

He bit her lower lip and tugged, sliding his tongue inside heaven. Her nails bit into his shoulder, and their tongues tangled in bliss. Her husky whimpers seemed to take hold of his groin and give a tug. Sweet mercy, he wanted her. His loins were aching and heavy, and he wanted to take her upstairs, strip her naked, worship her with open-mouthed, lascivious kisses against her wet sex, before burying his cock deep, and riding her for the night.

Lost in the haze of roaring needs and a burning desire he had been denying, he gripped her hips and positioned her, so she sat astride him. They broke apart, breathing raggedly, and peering into each other's eyes. For some reason he anticipated a slap to his cheek for his audacity. But his lovely Verity only stared at him, passionate shock in her golden eyes.

"I ache," she said softly.

The space between them heated, and his control wavered. "I burn."

Without breaking her gaze, he tightened his grip on her hips and rocked her down and over the hard ridge of his cock which strained against his trousers.

Her cheeks flushed, her lips parted, and her eyes widened. James did it again and a wild cry tore from her throat. Even through the layers of her gown and petticoats, she would feel the sensations as he slid her down, then up in a slow sensuous glide over the hardened length of his cock. Her eyes clouded with dazed delight, and something hungry throbbed inside of him to relinquish control and be the right kind of wicked.

He slid one of his hands down, dragging her dress and crinkling petticoats up as he stroked along her stocking-clad leg past her garter. He then wrapped his fingers around her bare thigh. The need that tore through him was a savage, demanding, relentless ache. His palm found the inside of her thigh, stroked, caressed, as he savored the feeling of her softness.

James fiercely reminded himself she had been through hell, a genteel lady who'd come to him for protection and he would not take advantage of her innocent sensuality. Not when enough men in her life had disappointed her.

She pressed a soft kiss to his lips. "I have never felt anything as beautiful as when you kissed me."

The softly whispered words cut through his heart and left him bleeding, vulnerable, and he did not like the need and uncertainty pouring through him. It felt like everything had change.

"Verity, I—"

With a choked sob of need, she thrust her fingers through his hair, lifting his face to her as she lowered hers to meet his lips. Her fists knotted in his hair, on his shoulders, at the small of his back as she became the ravisher and he the seduced. James fell under her spell, willingly, and it was he who became enslaved to the driving demands of her kisses which bespoke innocence and a wild, burgeoning passion.

A girl of less strength of character might have succumbed to seduction, burning in wild passion, without thoughts of consequences. But not his Verity. Another choked sob came from her and she shimmied off his lap to sit beside him. He braced for her to jump from the chaise and perhaps call him every deserving name in the book—a wicked seducer, a despoiler of innocents, a disgraceful libertine. She did neither, and an emotion he would never be able to quantify rose in his chest like a storm when she leaned to the side and rested her head against his shoulder.

"Will this brief moment of madness ruin our friendship?" she murmured huskily.

And somewhere inside he hurt, though he could not explain it in full. How happy he would have been if she had demanded that he paid a visit to her brother and did the honorable thing. For he would marry her…in a heartbeat. Would she resent him if he took the choice from her and called upon her brother?

A brief moment of madness. If he respected her and the choices she wanted to make for her life, he would have to chalk up their soul-shattering kisses to a moment of madness and nothing more. It was clear that was what she wanted. His stomach twisted in tight, painful knots. "Nothing could ruin our friendship." *It is too precious.* "We must simply ensure this…madness does not happen again."

She made no reply and he did not require one from her. They stayed like that for a few minutes, before he stood. Without question she followed him as he led her outside and into the carriage. Verity did not question it when he hauled himself inside the coach and sat on the squabs opposite to her.

James escorted her home, and they did so in silence. And when the coachman opened the carriage door and assisted her down, he watched as she disappeared into the safe haven of her home.

It was early yet, just midnight, perhaps he could visit the club or even White's. Yet James did neither. He went home, climbed into his bed, and dreamt of Lady Verity.

※

THREE DAYS HAD PASSED since Verity had been seared with desire, her world upended, her expectations of passion shattered and reshaped, by a kiss. She had not been able to stop thinking about the feel and taste of Lord Maschelly's mouth upon hers. For the dozenth time, she pressed trembling fingers to her lips and closed her eyes. She could still feel him there, a ghost determined to haunt her with wicked memories of passion and possibilities. Even when the marquess had kissed her before he had revealed himself a vile brute, she had never felt anything beyond mild frustration and annoyance for she had not found pleasure in his embrace.

Not so with James. There had only been desire. And most distressing of all...*I want you to kiss me again.* Did that make her a wanton…a tart? It had been a similar recklessness which had caused her to trust a blackguard and he had attacked her. What if—?

No! Something fierce and unexpected welled inside of Verity. *I shall not blame myself for his vile actions anymore.* And the earl would never force himself on her. The man had honor, and a kindness that was unmatched in anyone she knew.

But what did it mean that she wanted to kiss him again, perhaps even do more?

She sucked in a sharp breath, do more? *Oh, I am being a silly, silly miss!*

The door to the earl's townhouse opened unexpectedly, and the butler stared down at her with a baffled frown on his face. Verity blushed for she had been standing outside for at least five minutes, lost in thoughts and indecision. The butler possibly had been aware she stood outside, dreading seeing the earl after their encounter. Verity felt vexed she was already blushing, and she had not seen James as yet. It was a pity she could not retain her veil for the duration of today's lesson.

"My lady, please come inside."

She took a steady breath and stepped inside.

"May I take your coat my lady?"

With a nod, she unbuttoned her pelisse and handed it to Fenton.

"The ballroom has been prepared, if you will come this way, my lady."

She hesitated. "And is the earl in the ballroom?"

"No, milady. He is in the library. I will inform him you have arrived after I've escorted you."

"Thank you, Fenton," she said with a smile. "I will inform the earl I've arrived. Please do not trouble yourself." Verity could never abide *waiting* whenever she was overly anxious.

At the library, she knocked once, then opened the door and proceeded inside. James stood by the fireplace, dressed as a distinguished gentleman. Even the cravat seemed perfectly tied. He held a drink in his hand, and his face held an air of serious contemplation.

"A shilling for your thoughts, my lord," she said, trying to ignore the flutter of heat low in her stomach.

He leveled his regard on her. "You are wearing a dress."

She wore a sapphire blue evening gown, with matching gloves and delicate slippers. Her dress bared the creamy swell of her shoulders, her décolletage, and flattered her shape to its best advantage. Verity removed her hat and veil but kept them in her hand. "Ladies do tend to dance in these, you know, not trousers. I thought you would appreciate that bit of authenticity while we practice."

Despite her attempt at levity, there was a tension in the air, the memory of their passionate kisses in his eyes. Verity fought the heat rising in her cheeks and moved further into the room.

"You are *beautiful*."

That was almost said with a reverent whisper.

Considerably shaken, she shifted away so he could not see her expression of similar want, for there could be no mistaking the provocative desire in his brilliant eyes. Verity made her way over to the sofa and lowered herself. Folding her arms demurely in her lap, she said, "Compliments should be elegantly expressed. Your utterance just now was filled with too much passion…and would likely perturb a young lady."

James arched a brow. "I suspect you are not jesting."

Verity grinned. "I am not."

His penetrating gaze searched her face. "A lady would prefer practiced flattery instead of genuine admiration."

"Some."

"What do you prefer?"

His question flustered Verity, and it was a full minute before she was able to answer him with some semblance of composure. "I've never given it much thought."

His regard warmed with something teasing and tender. "Did you appreciate it when I told you just now, how exquisitely ravishing you are?"

She looked at him rather helplessly. "You said beautiful."

"They hold the same meaning," he said with a smile which crinkled the corner of his eyes.

"Yes," she said with a touch of asperity. "My heart jerked with a thrill I have never experienced in my entire life."

Verity bit back a smile as she realized, with satisfaction, that she had succeeded in discomfiting him. "Are you blushing, my lord?"

He scowled. "Of course not."

Yet there was the slightest tinge of flush along his rugged cheekbones. The notion she could ruffle the feathers of a man so self-assured sent a dizzying surge of warmth through her veins. She flashed a mischievous smile at him, and murmured, "Another lesson: compliments must not be overly bold or familiar lest the line of propriety is breached. They must be tender, subtle, yet artful."

"Lesson noted."

He prowled over to her and held out his hand. "Shall we dance?"

She allowed him to pull her up and she walked beside him in silence as they made their way to his ballroom. The space echoed with emptiness, but the scent on lemon wax was redolent on the air. It was quite a large ballroom with two folding doors which could open up to the larger drawing room. Floor to ceiling windows dominated a large portion of the room, and the gold and blue striped wallpaper lent the room an air of elegance. The room was brightly lit with several lamps and candles. Verity could imagine a ball here, thousands of candles lit on the chandeliers, the scent of lavender and honeysuckle filling the lungs, the laughter and chatter, and the music.

Verity spun to face him, trying not to blush at the intent way he stared at her. He was unpardonable in his admiration, and it was as if he memorized everything about her. A pang tore through her heart. Was he too dreading the day their clandestine lessons would end?

"You are the most graceful man I know."

"It is easy for me to deduce you socialize with few gentlemen."

"The fluidity of your movements when you teach me to fight, your stylishness as you dart and shift, at times you mesmerize me how light you are on your feet, James. You should take that same skill and passion into dance."

She sauntered over to him and placed the tip of her finger over his chest. *Tap. Tap. Tap.* "Feel the beat of the music here. You have the perfect elegance to dance the waltz."

As if he could not help himself, he drew her close and spun her so she stood by his side. She turned her head to look at him wonderingly. "You've had some lessons?" she asked archly.

"I admit it, I hired a tutor once."

They took three steps forward, and then faced each other.

"Can you imagine the strains of the orchestra?" she hummed slightly. "Can you hear it?"

"I believe I can."

"Then dance with me, James."

His eyes darkened, and he took her into the perfect position, sliding his arms along hers to hold her by the elbows, then tugging her into the invisible strains of the waltz. Verity hummed, and they glided around the room, at first with some measure of awkwardness and then with such commanding poise and agility he stole her breath. How long they rotated and spun she could not say, but when they halted, they were both laughing like dolts.

Looking up at him she clapped. "I have been deceived, James, you are a wonderful dancer! This lesson has been wonderfully diverting. Are you to attend Lady William's midnight ball in a few weeks? I daresay by then we should master the grand waltz, and the quadrille. It would be the perfect place to ask a young lady to dance, someone of your liking of course, and perhaps you should endeavor to pay her a compliment."

His grunt of irritation implied he was not in accord with that plan.

She sent him a perplexed glance. "Or perhaps not to dance?"

"The way we move together, Verity, I would be most astonished if such perfection could be accomplished with just anyone."

The unexpectedness of this admission took her breath away. "James…"

He bowed. "Accept my thanks for a most agreeable evening, Verity. I believe tonight's lesson has been imparted. I shall call the carriage for you."

Before she could question his sudden coolness, he'd already turned away, making his way for the entrance. She stared at his retreating back, an unknown hunger crawling through her. And at its heart there was also a sadness.

What do you want from me, James? And why do I want to give it to you, more than I've wanted anything in my whole life?

CHAPTER 10

Six weeks and two days had passed since Verity had appeared on the earl's doorstep. She had been instructed several times thus far in the art of fighting, and she had been horrified this morning to note the slight development of muscles in her upper arms. She felt fitter, more confident, and less afraid. It was as if with each lesson, she vanquished the lingering dread.

Their unorthodox friendship flourished with each titillating secretive encounter, and Verity's admiration for James grew to an astonishing degree. A gentleman is thought to be of top quality through education, refinement, polished manners, a considerable degree of charm, and the productive management of his inheritance. With each passing reflection, which Verity admitted was terribly often, she'd deduced James was *more* than a gentleman.

He truly existed in a class of his own, and the appellation could not stand alone to describe James. He was charming, kind, thoughtful in his manners and civility, yet at times mercurial and abrupt, with layers to his character Verity presumed would take her years to understand. He challenged her, encouraged her, and always lent a listening ear whenever she vented her frustration of the tiresome nature of the season's frivolities, the gossip sheets, and the hurtful distance with her family.

Verity waited for the earl in his brightly lit library. A decanter of sherry had been rested on the mantle along with whisky. She removed her hat and veil and lowered herself into the plush sofa. She had arrived at James's townhouse at her usual time, but he had not been present. That had been a first. Tonight's lesson was to be a continuation of the art of intelligent conversations with a lady of society. This had proven the most challenging aspect to James, for he wished to discuss politics, past wars, the economy, horse racing, and even fishing.

When she had suggested he could soften the tension by commenting on the weather, his muttered, "Good God!" had been filled with such horror she had laughed and admitted such conversation could be intolerable but seemed to be the expected norm. That evening they had engaged in such lively discourse, the night had ended without their lesson.

That was becoming too common, and she was determined to honor her part of the bargain. Even though the awareness of what he might do with the knowledge hurt somewhere deep inside. The ending of their arrangement hovered. Only last week they had decided to reduce how often she sneaked away from her home to be with him. Mamma and Albert were becoming irritated with her various excuses to be absent from social events.

There had been a rout-party last week, Albert had been most adamant she should attend. Verity went and had been alarmed that her brother was seeking a political connection with the hostess's father. The man had to be thrice Verity's age! The pressure from her brother to depart his household had increased dramatically, and the sense that she ought to find a gentleman to her liking and be pleasantly receptive to his advances lurked in her convictions.

Yet, Verity only saw James. Her nights were no longer beset by terrible nightmares. All dreams led to James's kisses and sometimes eccentric charm. Charms he would use to woo a lady of quality. With a scowl, Verity dismissed thoughts of James courting another lady, and opened a copy of a gothic which she had plucked earlier from his extensive library. The clock on the mantle struck, and she glanced up. It was almost nine. Footsteps echoed in the hallway, and she lowered the book as the door opened.

"Forgive my tardiness," he said brusquely. "I had another matter to attend."

"James is all well?" she enquired, noting the slight stiffness in his frame.

He raked his fingers through his hair, and there was an air of anger surrounding him. "Well enough. I believe we should allow for this lesson another time. It is already too late."

She stood, frowning at his dismissive manner, and moved closer to him. Verity stared at his hands. "Upon my word, James, you are bleeding!"

She hurried over to him and grabbed his hand, lifting it for her inspection. With rough irritation, he pulled it from her. "It is nothing!"

"I can't for the life of me conceive why you are acting so boorish," she snapped sharply. "Please tell me what happened?"

"I was in a fight," he replied with curt incivility.

"And?"

A scowl darkened his face. "There is no more."

Verity dropped his hand with an irritated huff, ambled to the mantle and poured whisky into a glass. Once back at his side, she reached into his top pocket for his handkerchief. "You have worn my patience very thin already, please be more forthcoming."

"There is a man, Lord Newsome…"

"Viscount Newsome?"

"The very one," James said dryly. "Last week he met in a carriage accident. He was reckless and drunk, driving at an alarming speed. A woman was killed. He was at the club today, laughing over the matter."

Verity gasped. "I cannot credit such abominable behavior!"

"He was next in the fighting pits, and I went in and challenged him. After calling him a stain on humanity. I thrashed him soundly." He glanced down at his bruised and bleeding fists. "I did not even take the time to wrap my hands. Sometimes I wonder if I seek any excuse to fight. I've not needed the money made from such fights in more than three years. But I find myself returning over and over."

She lifted his knuckle closer to the lamp, dipped the handkerchief into the whisky, and dabbed it on the torn flesh. A hiss of pain slipped from him, but she did not slow her ministrations, cleaning away the blood. "Do you wish to stop? Fighting that is?"

He considered this, his eyes shuttering. "Whenever I step in the ring, there is always a wave of anger in me…it feels dark, a living entity, and being in the ring, somehow suppresses it. I crave the pleasure of tangling with an opponent who is worthy."

"You have too much honor and kindness in you, James, for me to believe you only fight for the thrill of it."

He peered down at her with a surprised mien.

She cleaned away all the blood from his hands and rested the cloth and empty whisky glass on the table, before facing him once more. "Do you think I have not seen your character? You have enfolded me under your protective wings, for *little* in return, because in your heart you are already a gentleman. And I suspect you know it, James. You helped me simply because you want to see me bloom," she whispered achingly. "What manner of man acts like this? One who has honor and courage, and all the fine qualities my papa would say were tip-top."

"How are you so sweet?" he demanded gruffly.

"I eat a lot of delicacies and cakes."

A snort sounded. "You are also silly. But I like it."

"Somehow I am gathering you believe this to be flattery?"

"Yes," he retorted, without an instant's hesitation.

"It's the most absurd and inelegant compliment," she agreed mischievously. "My lessons are failing."

He thought for a few moments. "Your eyes are as brown as mud but *prettier*. Your lips are as thick..."

Verity choked on her laughter. "Thick? We have spent so many hours reading Lord Byron, John Blunt, and…and…" she broke off giggling.

"Oh? What is this delightful, girlish laugh I hear?" Then he acted as if he caught the sound and placed it over his heart.

She sobered and stared at him, desperately wishing for his kiss. "We are good friends aren't we, James?" *Do not be a silly goose and ruin it*, she reminded herself fiercely. Friends did not go around kissing each other.

He looked at her in surprise, and then, after a moment, smiled. "As unlikely as it seems, Verity, we are."

He unexpectedly curved his arm around her shoulders and dragged her against the solid wall of his chest…into a hug. Verity waited for him to lift her chin and place his lips to hers. Instead of the kiss she had anticipated, his fingers lightly traced her cheek. Her pulse pounded, and she felt confused by the breathless sensations tumbling through her heart. She pressed her face even more against his chest, wishing she could stay there forever. The thought so startled her she pulled away, putting a respectable distance between them.

He rubbed the back of his neck, a too heavy sigh slipping from him. "I am weary."

She paused at the admission. "I shall take my leave. Perhaps we may have our lesson tomorrow then." And she wondered then for how long they would prolong this charade.

As if he had peeked into her mind he said, "It is time we pick a date to end our lessons, Verity. We have been taking an enormous gamble with your reputation for over a month, and I would be a reprobate to keep us on this path."

"Am I getting to be a good fighter then?" she demanded archly.

"You are incredible."

And that left her speechless for his tone echoed with such genuine admiration. All the possible replies running through her mind felt useless, so she made no reply. Verity collected her reticule and hat with veil.

"Stay."

"Only for a few minutes."

And she stayed for an hour, curled into the softness of the sofa, while the earl sat in the high-backed chair before the fire, his legs sprawled in front of him, gazing into the flames. During which time Verity had her book open, reading into the stillness of the night, ignoring the lump forming in her throat and the unusual ache stirring in her soul for James.

※

LADY WILLIAM's ball was a crushing success. Laughter and facile conversation floated on the air, and the vividly colored ball gowns, dancing slippers, diamonds, pearls, and rubies shone iridescently under the candlelight of the crystal chandeliers in the glittering ballroom. Verity had been at the ball for more than two hours, and the heat of the packed ballroom was stifling. James was in attendance, but they had carefully maintained a distance. She had not been introduced to him, and he had not sought it.

James mingled with the crowd, and from the many smiles and approving nods, Verity suspected he charmed them. The dowager duchess of Middleton introduced him to her daughter, whom if Verity recalled correctly, was nineteen, and an heiress. Soon James was leading the Lady Anna to the dance floor, his poise one of supreme confidence. He was beautiful, in a way that was uniquely male, and she was not the only lady noticing. Many not on the dance floor discreetly watched the earl and Lady Anna as they twirled to the sensually freeing waltz. For such a large man he appeared light and graceful on his feet, and Lady Anna's face glowed as she peered up at him. Many in society noted it was the earl's very first dance, the whispers buzzed and speculation grew.

"It's his first dance of the season!"
"They do look splendid together."

WHEN THE EARL WAS WICKED

"The rumor says he is looking to settle down."

"Perhaps there is some sort of tendre, and they've been very circumspect about it!"

Many fans were opened, and the whispers abounded. The speculation would also spill onto the scandal sheets and newspapers. Verity knew what they all wondered. Why was Lord Maschelly paying attention to Lady Anna Covington? Did they sense a match in the air?

"There is a rumor he offered for the silly girl, and she refused him? An earl believed to have an income of fifty thousand a year, and one so very large and handsome."

This was murmured with an undertone of envy and frustration.

Verity glanced at Lady Susanna, to whom that particular piece of fluff referred. Susanna stared at James and Lady Anna with an expression akin to envy. And Verity felt a pang of regret for her. The more she watched James dance, a hollow sensation burrowed its way into her heart, and she admitted she wished with every fiber of her being he was dancing with her... soaring across the expanse of the dance floor.

"Your earl is quite dashing and very different tonight," Caroline said, coming to stand beside her and looping their hands together. "He is normally often brusque to the point of incivility at these events! But now he is positively charming everyone! Even the Grande Dame has smiled at him. Can you imagine that querulous biddy smiling?"

Verity laughed at Caroline's silliness.

"You are being excessively impertinent, Caroline," Verity warned.

"They would not suit," her friend whispered.

Verity glanced around. "Who?"

Caroline's eyes lit with mischief and a good deal of speculation. "Lord Maschelly and Lady Anna. I am sure there isn't anyone more amiable and obliging than Lady Anna. That man…is a lion. And he will need a fiery and feisty lady to walk by his side. Say, like one who has been spending an inordinate amount of time with him, and who is not afraid to learn to fight."

Verity flushed and ignored that pointed bid for more information. Feeling in need of a breath of fresh air, she promised Caro to see her before leaving. Verity then discreetly left the public rooms and made her way to the smaller drawing room which had not been opened specifically to the guests. She went over opening the tall French doors that led outside and toward the gardens at the back of the townhouse. The paths were well lit with lanterns, but empty of guests. There was a small alcove at the end, with a fountain, and a bench. Once there, she breathed a soft sigh of relief to be away from the stifling heat, and the surprising pain of seeing James touching, and smiling down at another lady. In the privacy of the alcove, it was hard to stop the lone tear which slid down her cheek.

"Verity."

She gasped, pressing a hand to her chest, and glanced up. "James! I hadn't thought anyone would notice I slipped away. The crush is so overwhelming, and everyone was so diverted by the entertainment."

"You were discreet, I was simply aware of you," he murmured, the gleam in his eyes hard to interpret. "I am sorry I frightened you."

He sat beside her on the stone bench, staring into the surprisingly clear star-studded night.

Did he feel the same longing she endured? Or did James only see them as friends? These were questions she longed to ask, but did not broach, for his answer had the power to wound her heart. Verity had tried to examine the feelings she owned for the man before her, but she had been unable to shape them into any semblance of clarity.

She placed her hand in the small space between them, and he covered it with his. Even through the gloves they wore, she could feel the warm vitality of James. She was very much aware of the strength and power of the shoulder that flexed each time he shifted, as if restless.

"May I kiss you, Verity?"

The earth shifted and took very precious moments to align. "And we return to friends in the morning?" she asked in a deliberately thoughtful tone.

Her pulse had quickened alarmingly, she felt achy, terrifyingly breathless and she struggled to retain her equanimity. She had always believed that once she met the man she would eventually marry, she would recognize him immediately. His affability, polished manners, humorous anecdotes would have instantly captured her attention and heart. It had been the reason she had not been overly interested in any of the four suitors her brother had lured her way since the start of the season. They had been handsome, wealthy, amiable, and they had lavished her with extravagant praise and flattery. But Verity had been unmoved, and quite confident none of them would become her future husband.

And then, James…

The rumble of his voice pierced the frantic whirl of her thoughts.

"Yes, we shall still be friends in the morning."

She parted her lips to ask if he ever dreamt of more and was beset by such shyness and nerves she trembled. "Then it is perfectly permissible to kiss me," she said huskily, even knowing his touch would evoke chaotic desires and wants she would not understand.

He gathered her into his arms and kissed her: Softly…hesitantly and then with domineering tenderness. He coaxed her lips to part with nips and huskily murmured nonsense. She pleaded for more when he slowed his ravishment, and he rewarded her with even deeper kisses. Their tongues tangled, their moans merged, and greed flamed through Verity's soul.

They broke apart, breathing raggedly. A sharp awareness filled her. "This felt like a farewell, James."

"Only to our clandestine meetings. We shall see each other quite often about town."

Disappointment swept through her like a chill. There was more twisting under the surface of her skin, but she could not examine it at this moment.

She leaned forward and pressed a kiss against his cheek.

"Thank you, James. I am excessively obliged to you, and shall never forget your kindness."

He pressed a kiss to her forehead. "Perhaps one last lesson."

Regret and something undefinable throbbed in his tone. Verity smiled, the ache in her heart soothed from the heavy sadness in his tone.

"Perhaps one more."

CHAPTER 11

James had not thought there was anything under the sun which could have distracted him from thinking about Lady Verity. For the last three days and nights, she haunted his dreams. And he watched the setting and the rising of the sun as if that would make Monday's session arrive any sooner. Their last lesson.

Twice they had now kissed. And the word 'kiss' seemed quite pedantic to describe the event which had unfolded last night, and that day in his library. She inspired him to compose poetry—admittedly, all his writings would all be wicked reminiscence of the softness and the plumpness of her lips, the sweetness of her tongue, and those delectable whimpering noises of passion she made so breathlessly against his mouth. Not the muddled nonsense he had teased her with.

What did *she* think of their illicit embraces?

He wanted to lay her atop his sheets, naked, and lick and suck every inch of her body, bringing her to pleasure over and over. Did she hunger for more as he did? Of course, she would not be thinking of him in a similarly wicked manner. She was intelligent, amusing, and a lady of thoughtful manners. Not a delectable tart who would willingly be wanton with him between the sheets, and perhaps, in the library on the rug by a fire. Or even the desk before which he now sat. The broad surface filled his imagination with endless possibilities. James had never felt this way about a lady before in all his eight and twenty years; and instinct warned him, this was rare and precious.

With a groan, he sank back even further into the high winged back chair. Lady Verity was solely for marriage. A piercing yearning went through him for her. Though she appeared so delicate at times, she had never flinched from him or made him feel as if he were a damned brute.

She looked at him with trust…and passion, and he hoarded the memory of every smile she had ever bestowed upon him. What he hated the most was the shadow of pain which still lingered in her eyes. James wanted to be the one to lay her dreams at her feet and be the slayer of her nightmares. But what did she want? *Merciful Christ.* Never had he wished he understood the female mind more? Somehow, he did not believe if he were to call upon her home, as a suitor, she would be receptive of such advances. The lady had made it clear the kind of gentleman she wished to marry, and James was certain, though she liked and admired him, and even trusted in their budding relationship, the lady did not think of him for marriage.

These were the ruminations which had occupied his mind for the last hour. For days he had not been able to stop thinking about her. Must be some sorcery.

James's man of affairs, Mr. Everton Powell, interrupted his musings and presented him with a box. It flummoxed James that the man had had to clear his throat three times to fully capture his attention. Even then, half of his thoughts had been on Verity, recalling her smile and how beautiful she had appeared at the ball last night. *Should I send her flowers?*

"My lord," said Mr. Powell, clearing his throat. "I did not look inside the box, but I thought it wise to bring it to you since it had…the late countess's name written on the side."

With those cryptic words, James's attention was finally free of Verity's beguiling sorcery. This box had his mother's name. "You said this was found in the wine cellar?"

"Yes, my lord. Repairs have only recently started there."

James nodded. The estate on which he had grown, or near where he had grown, Birchmount Manor—the seat of his earldom and the place where his father had sequestered himself until his death. James had always roamed those walls, feeling hurt and angry that there was no portrait of his mother, and that he could not live at the last place she had resided. Many of the villagers had believed in spirits, and they had regaled him with dozens of stories. And the foolish hope in his heart had made him fervently think that if he could just live at the manor and avoid his father in the large one hundred room home, he would sense something of her presence. And maybe he could have asked her a question which had lingered in his young mind for so long. Did she hate him and blame him for her death as his father had done?

"Was anything else found with her name?"

"No, my lord. After we found this, Mrs. Thompson gathered the servants and had the manor searched from top to bottom."

Warmth filled James. Mrs. Thompson, the manor's cook, had been one of his fiercest champions growing up and had been a listening ear to many of his musings. She had also been the first person to attempt to teach him his letters.

"And, how is she?"

The man cleared his throat. "If I am permitted to say so, my lord, she misses you."

James nodded. He hadn't returned to Dorset in almost six years. Every brutal fight and purse he had won had been pushed into restoring those neglected lands and tenants' houses. Thousands of pounds had been invested into new types of machinery for the farmers, larger houses, a village school, fixing and expanding the church, and to commission a hospital. He had never forgotten those he had cared for dying from various diseases, waiting for a doctor to visit from a nearby village. He had sweated blood and tears for the people who had grown him, yet he had not returned since he left.

"I promise a visit soon."

"Yes, my lord. The repairs on Birchmount

Manor should be completed in less than two weeks, my lord. Every room has been restored to its former glory, the furniture refurbished and restored. The silverware replaced. The servants walk with pride in their steps."

"Thank you, Mr. Powell. That will be all."

The man departed, and James stared at the box for an inordinate amount of time. He hadn't hungered for knowledge of his mother for years. Not when it had all seemed so futile. He had several different descriptions of her from the villages, yet it had not been enough for him to paint a picture of her. He knew she was kind. So all the tenants had said. She would attend to them often, brought the poorer villagers food and medicine. And she loved to sing. James sounded like a frog whenever he attempted it, so he knew he did not get that talent from her.

But he loved the pianoforte, and he heard from the housekeeper more than once his mother's skill had been unmatched.

He turned the box almost idly, wondering if he was afraid of opening it. The wild scrawl of her name on the box was in his father's handwriting. James could almost sense the rage and pain that had been in his father as he wrote the letters.

For the first time in years, and perhaps ever, he felt a pang of sympathy. James suspected he was falling in love with Lady Verity's charming wit and fierce spirit. How long had he known her? A few weeks? And the knowledge if harm were to befall her it would ravage somewhere deep inside of him sat on his shoulder.

His father had fallen in love with his mother and married her. He'd had her for a little over ten years before he lost her, but he must have loved her with a depth and breadth little would comprehend. James had been in the room when his father had laid dying.

"Georgiana," James whispered, saying the name his father had cried, right before he had smiled and gone onto his rewards.

He traced the name on the box. *Georgiana*. With a muttered oath and great annoyance at his prevarication, he wrenched the lid off the box. The first sight that greeted him was a white blanket, with blue trimmings. He took it up, and a pleasant scent of lavender hit his senses and sent him reeling.

Why was a blanket at the top of the box? He flashed it open, and something tugged his attention to the edge. It was an embroidered name: James.

He took a deep breath and glanced into the

box. There he spied a small brown book, well five of them, tied with a red ribbon. He untied the strip and took up the first book and opened it. A diary and it was hers. He sat heavily into his chair and started to read.

Dearest Diary,

I met the most wonderful, amiable, and so very handsome young man today. Our meeting was by happenstance. He knocked into me as I exited the library and knocked over my package of books. He apologized so charmingly as he gathered them for me. At least four times. I had to reassure him he did no harm, and I cannot explain how my heart pounded in his presence. Somehow neither of us thought to affect introductions, so caught up we were on staring into each other's eyes. How gloriously alive I felt. And how happy I had followed mamma and Judith to town for the season. I usually find balls so intolerably dull, but that day my boredom vanished. My dear friend, Theodosia, told me he is the Earl of Maschelly, and he had only recently inherited the earldom, and that he is seeking a wife! Wouldn't it be just wonderful if he considered me?

The joy infused in the words said so much about her character. A wound he thought he had long closed, burst open, and that keen sense of loss, and hope that he would one day know her scythed through his heart. Hours passed in the library as he pored over her journal. He was there on the journey as she attended lavish balls after balls, dancing with his father, their first scandalous kiss. Then their marriage, and her pregnancy.

James's heart kicked when he saw his name in a passage that had started with her wondering if she would birth a boy or a girl.

> *I know you to be a boy, my darling. I am so confident about it, and I shall call you James. We cannot wait to meet you. After ten years of wonderful marriage, I am finally fulfilling my duty. I am eager to hold you in my arms and kiss your forehead. Your powerful kicks tell me you will have your father's size—*

Christ. He slammed the diary shut. His father's size. James glanced down at his hand. Had she known to birth him would have taken her life? He glanced back at the diary. Of course not, each word had been filled with hope and love. And he was glad she'd had that rare kind of love in her life. And she had loved him before he had even born.

He reached for the stack of letters and opened

one. James frowned. They were all pleading letters from Mrs. Judith Brimley. After reading several letters, he realized Mrs. Brimley was his mother's sister and his aunt. Shock robbed him of breath for several moments. He had a family he did not know about? The last letter had been sent eleven years ago from an address in Hampshire. Had she sent more letters since? His father had only died seven years past. James gathered from the tone of the letters, which enquired after his health with pleadings for her to visit, she had never received a response.

How cruel his father had been in his grief. Packing away everything into the box, he rose and made his way from the library to his room. There he dismissed his startled valet and lay atop his sheets fully clothed. The emotions in his heart could not be fully understood by James. They were a tangled mess of anger, sadness, and hope. He closed his eyes, and it felt like hours later before he was finally able to fall asleep to the memory of Verity laughing and dancing in his arms.

EARLY THE VERY NEXT MORNING, before the dawn had broken, James was on his way to Hampshire in

WHEN THE EARL WAS WICKED

a carriage pulled by his fastest horses. He had sent a cautious note to Lady Verity, canceling their lesson for the upcoming week. James had not provided an explanation, but he had apologized, knowing how much their sessions meant to her. The journey down was uneventful and took him two days at the pace he traveled. He stayed overnight at inns and was on his way again before the sun rose. After arriving at the return address on the letters, the butler informed him the master of the manor was not at home, and that Mrs. Brimley resided at a cottage about a mile away.

James wasted no time pondering why his aunt had moved and arrived at a modest cottage with the loveliest garden he had ever seen at about two in the afternoon. He dismounted from his carriage and noted no stable lad appeared to offer water or oats for the horses. In fact, he spied no stables. The gravel crunched under his feet as he walked along the driveway, up the few front steps, and knocked on the door.

It took a few moments before a rosy-cheeked, rotund woman opened it. She stared at him and then at the well-sprung carriage behind him.

"May I help you, Sir?" she asked a mite nervously.

"I am here to see Mrs. Judith Brimley. I've no appointment, but if you tell her Lord Maschelly has called, I would appreciate it."

Flustered the lady stepped back and beckoned for him to follow her. James was escorted to a small but tastefully furnished parlor—a pianoforte and a harp were positioned near a small chaise; the dark damask sofa matched the red and peach patterned wallpapers and drapes which covered the floor to ceiling windows. It was only upon close inspection one would notice the furniture and carpets had the appearance of shabby gentility.

When Mrs. Judith Brimley entered her small but tasteful parlor, James glanced up. She paused, a hand fluttering to her chest.

"There is no mistake you are the earl," she said after a minute of staring.

And standing before the fireplace, he was aware of how he would appear to her—a powerfully built man with dark hair, and a swarthy complexion.

A pleased smile settled on her lovely countenance, and she advanced further into the room. When she made to dip into a curtsy, he stopped her.

"Please, let's not stand on formality."

She beamed at him, and he couldn't help staring at her loveliness.

"This is indelicate of me, but might I enquire of your age, Mrs. Brimley?"

Verity would have scolded him for his forward and ungentlemanly manners.

"Please call me Judith…or Aunt Judith if you would prefer," she said hesitantly, and with such a hopeful air, he disguised the shock of emotions her word elicited.

"Perhaps Judith for now?"

Her smile got even brighter, for his familiarity showed he was willing to accept a degree of intimacy. "I am four and fifty."

"And still one of the loveliest ladies my eyes have ever beheld," he said with soft charm, thinking how pleased Verity would be with his compliment. It had come from a genuine place inside, and he couldn't help wondering if Judith and his mother bore any resemblance.

She flushed and patted her hair with self-conscious charm. They sat on the sofa closest to the windows overlooking the beautiful gardens.

"Forgive me for arriving without advance notice."

Her eyes brimmed with unexpected tears.

"Think nothing of it. I have been waiting eight and twenty years to meet my sister's child."

He cleared his throat. "I never knew you existed," he offered, as a way to soothe the hurt glaring from green eyes so very much like his own.

His aunt's tears spilled over. Discomfited at the sight, and unsure what comfort to offer, James withdrew his handkerchief and handed it to her. She dabbed at her eyes and breathed in shakily. Then she told him of his mother, a young lady from a family of gentry which had ties to nobility through an uncle who was a baronet, before she had fallen in love with the earl.

"Their love was a scandal of sorts, a match of the season, an evident love match. Though through her marriage my prospects for a good marriage improved considerably, I moved with her to Birchmount Manor because we were best of friends. I lived with Gina—"

"Gina?"

"It is what we called her growing up. I stayed with her from when I was seventeen until her death."

James flinched, and she leaned forward and patted his arms reassuringly. "She had a good life, a blessed life I would say, and she was deliriously happy. After…after she had gone to her rewards the earl banished me from Birchmount Manor. At that time I was six and twenty, a spinster, without many prospects, but I made a good match only a few months later with a most wonderful gentleman. We had twenty good years and two fine daughters."

"I have cousins?"

"Yes, Alice is seventeen and Eleanor nineteen. They are lovely girls, however overly inquisitive and have been known to act without decorum and eavesdrop at doors."

Muffled laughter sounded, then footsteps were heard scampering away.

"Please forgive their impertinence," she said, flushing.

James smiled. "Think nothing of it. I am looking forward to meeting them."

They spoke at length of his father's refusal to have her at the manor, and the several times she had been turned away when she had ventured there without an invitation. His father had shut everyone out in his grief. James sensed if he told her of his harsh and neglected upbringing, she would blame herself unjustly for not trying with more diligence to see him. Eventually, he would tell her a bit of his youth, when they had formed a much closer relationship, and he could assess the strength of her character, for he would not burden her when there was no need.

"And what of your husband?"

Pain darkened her eyes. "My Giles died a little over a year and a half ago."

And it was then he noticed her dress was a dark bombazine gown. "I am deeply sorry."

"We have rallied, and I daresay the girls shall be fine."

He glanced around the parlor once more, it testified to how much they have been struggling. "Did my mother get a chance to look upon me or did she pass immediately after birthing me?"

His unexpected question froze his aunt.

He raked a hand through his hair. "I found some diaries, and she had so looked forward to seeing me…I wondered if she got the chance," he said gruffly, a bit embarrassed by his sentimentality.

Judith's eyes softened with sympathy. "My dear boy, your mother had not died a few minutes after birthing you," she said. "But three days later."

"She suffered?" he demanded hoarsely.

"The opposite. I had never seen her happier."

Confusion rushed through him. "I do not understand."

"It was the childbed fever which took her. But in those three days, for hours she held you in her arms and sang. Whenever you cried, all she had to do was sing, and you would fall into a contented sleep. She died in her sleep, with a smile on her face, and I cannot help think it was thoughts of you and the earl who had comforted her."

"My father believed my size killed her."

She gasped. "Rubbish! In my experience, childbed fever can happen with babes of any size. Your father was a wounded lion, and nothing could have made him better. Only Georgiana, and she was gone from him."

The oddest sensation tugged deep inside of him. "Thank you for telling me."

His aunt smiled. "I am glad you got my letters."

They spoke well into the afternoon. He then met his two cousins who were quite lovely, having taken after their mother. Their excitement to meet him had been contagious, and he had found himself chatting quite comfortably with them when he had always been a man who was reserved with new acquaintances. He learned the girls had not come out and had never been to London since they did not possess land or dowry to attract any suitors. The cottage they now lived in had not been the one they had grown up in, but their father's heir, a distant cousin, had removed them from their home once he took possession. They had been living a retrenched life on a small widow's portion, which had been bequeathed to Judith. He was invited to stay for dinner which he accepted, and by the end of the meal, James had persuaded his aunt and cousins to live with him in London, permanently.

CHAPTER 12

Verity smiled at the charming young man who bowed over her gloved hands. He was barely an inch or two above her in height, his manners were pleasing, unpretentious, civil, and she did not feel threatened by him in any way. This man, Viscount Stanhope, had a distinguished reputation and was considered the first cut of a gentleman. His estates boasted an income of over thirty thousand pounds a year, a rumor existed he was overly generous with his servants, and he was in want of a wife. Many maters and their daughters had fluttered when he'd entered Lady Prendergast's ballroom, dreams of being his viscountess filling their hearts.

"Will you honor me with a dance, Lady Verity?

I have been told the waltz will be announced now," he murmured with a good-natured smile as he rose from his bow.

She dipped into a curtsy. "I would be delighted, my lord." And she allowed him to escort her toward the dancefloor. He had been at the ball for over two hours, and Verity was the only person he'd asked to dance for the evening. Several brows rose at that significant action. Lord Stanhope was the ideal type of gentleman she had planned to set her cap for, yet as Verity strolled onto the dancefloor with him, she felt no sense of thrill or anticipation.

Her thoughts were simply too occupied with missing James. It had been a full week since James had disappeared. His note had been infused with a sense of cryptic urgency.

Dear Vincent,

At first, she had grinned at that salutation. And she understood that greeting, for if his note had been intercepted, the reader would assume it was delivered to the wrong address.

I regret I must cancel our lesson for the foreseeable future.

That part had filled her with alarm and confusion. Whatever did he mean? Had it been their kiss the night before and the wicked and scandalous way she had clung to his shoulders? Or had it been her wanton entreaty for more? Just recalling it brought a flush to her cheeks.

There is a matter I must deal with that cannot be delayed. I apologize and will speak with you upon my return.

Yours, J.

Upon his return? Had the man left London? Of course, no answer had presented itself to her silent questions. And there had been an odd sense of hurt that he had not provided more information. She had berated herself sharply for her silliness. He owed her no explanation for there was no understanding between them. Yet, she thought their present friendship would have allowed for such confidences. She rested many of her dreams and burdens upon his shoulders in the fascinating conversations they had.

Exactly nine days had passed, and the man had not the decency to write and inform her if he was well. Vexation had settled in her heart, and she would not forgive him anytime soon for making her worry.

Are you well, James?

She pushed him from her mind as she danced with the viscount. They engaged in banal conversation which she did not mind, though she was a little bored. A few times the viscount made her laugh as he recounted tales from his travels to India. When the dance was over, he escorted her to the side and offered to fetch her some punch. Verity thanked him with a smile, and he wove through the throng toward the refreshment table.

A finger brushed over her elbow from behind, and a shiver of distaste crawled over her flesh. Swallowing back the nerves and awful feeling pitting in her stomach, Verity turned and peered up into the eyes of Lord Durham. Her brother stood beside him, and Albert smiled at her as if he saw nothing wrong with his actions.

"My dear sister, you remember my friend Lord Durham? Only this afternoon in the club the marquess and I reminisced about the times we spent together in friendship in Bedfordshire."

The marquess bowed briefly. "Will you honor

me with this next dance, Lady Verity?" he asked with charming amiability.

Her civility and the fact so many in the *ton* stared obliged her to say what was proper. "Lord Durham," she murmured. "I must decline. I feel as if I am about to vomit. A distemper of the stomach."

His lips tightened for a moment before he said, "Perhaps a walk on the terrace? I feel we have not conversed for a while, and dear Albert would like for us to be friends once more."

Several other couples and matrons lined the terrace, and they would be in full view, so anything improper was unlikely to occur. But she could not bear it. How dare he approach her in this manner? As if his terrible actions should be forgotten and forgiven. Verity realized her brother believed he was fixing a quarrel that had existed merely for far too long. The dispassionate disrespect to her pain made her want to howl her agony.

She leaned in slightly, lowering her voice so only the Marquess could hear. "I would rather kiss a snake."

The marquess stiffened, his eyes snapping with anger. "Your sister is quite uncivil with an unbecoming tongue," he drawled cuttingly to Albert.

Verity smiled. "And do not forget it, you pig!"

A flush ran along the marquess's face, and she could feel his anger. In his eyes, she saw that it was the public setting which saved her from his fury. She stepped back a few paces.

Her brother had the nerve to send her a disapproving glance, one which promised a strict private set down. "Verity—" he began warningly.

She turned around and pushed through the crowd, unable to bear being in their presence a second longer. Up ahead, she spied Duchess Carlyle and Viscountess Shaw in animated conversation. Verity would join them and prayed the marquess did not trouble her for the rest of the night. How she hated that her fingers trembled, and her heart raced. And she sensed in her dreams tonight, there would be an emergence of the nightmares.

A feeling of despair came over her, and she resiliently pushed it away. *Courage…Verity, Courage.*

HIS VERITY APPEARED RESPLENDENT, sheathed in a full yellow gown that flattered her lush frame to its exquisite advantage. Elbow-length white gloves covered her hands with sleek suppleness, and matching yellow dancing slippers encased her elegant feet. Her dark hair was caught atop her head in a riot of curls, a brilliant sapphire necklace encircled her throat, and matching earbobs winked at her ears. She was striking in her loveliness.

Beauty like the night.

He'd only just returned from Hampshire this evening, and he had been urged to attend tonight's ball by a driving impulse and a hope that he would see her. A rush of pleasure filled James's heart as he peered at Verity again, and he knew at that moment he would marry her or none at all. He would resort to using all the wicked charms he was so blithely told he possessed to convince her there was more than friendship between them. He could be all that she desired and more.

James moved down the stairs at a leisurely pace, keeping track of her almost frantic progress through the crowded ballroom. He frowned, belatedly realizing her agitation. Someone followed her, and he recognized Lord Durham, heir to the dukedom of Hartington. His father had been ill for some time, and the news about town was that the man would not live out the year. Instead of Durham sitting by his father's side, he was about town racing and gambling quite heavily on the promise he would be the duke soon.

Ice congealed inside James, as Durham watched Verity with single-minded concentration. The marquess ignored all attempts of those who tried to gain his attention, his regard only for Verity.

She chose that moment to glance up, and she flushed when she recognized James. Her entire face glowed with the prettiness of her smile, and the joy she found in seeing him. It almost became impossible to breathe, so visceral was the hunger dancing through his soul. He lifted his chin, the motion quick and discreet, indicating the exit of the ballroom leading to the hallway.

She changed her path, moving with discreet surety through the crowd. Only one person observed her, and he followed. James thrust through the crowd with little finesse, ignoring those who nodded at him and tried to capture his attention. Verity disappeared from the ballroom, and soon so did the marquess. James wanted to snarl as the crush impeded how fast he tried to move. Finally, he was in the hallway, he broke into a run, and then skidded to a stop when he came upon Verity leaning against the wall of the hall, with the marquess standing only a few feet from her, his face mottled with anger.

"How dare you try to slight me!" the man snarled.

She paled for a moment, her lower lip trembling before she lifted her chin. "If I have no wish to dance with a *rapist*, that is my choice."

Disbelief shot through James as the marquess lifted his hand and stepped forward threateningly.

A throb of violence poured through him in relentless waves. "If you take another step, I will break your goddamn arms!"

The marquess spun around, allowing his arm to drop. "Maschelly," he said, tugging at his cravat. "You interrupted a private moment with a…a friend."

"You were about to hit Lady Verity," James said, shocked at the man's arrogance and calm brutality. They were in a public setting, and the man would have placed his hands on her and remained confident that there was nothing she could do about it. The one person residing in her life left to defend and protect her honor had failed to do so repeatedly.

"What I was about to do is not your concern, Maschelly," Durham said coolly.

Within two strides he stood in front of the marquess, grabbed him by his collar, and slammed him into the wall with barely restrained fury.

"James!" Verity gasped, her eyes widening with her alarm.

"My word what is happening here?" a lady's voice gasped before she hurried away. No doubt to summon someone.

Verity hurried to him and touched his hand briefly. "Please, James. Not here. Do you want to start a scandal? May we just leave?"

He roughly pushed the marquess away from him, and all the man did was fix his cravat, his eyes narrowing on them.

"I wonder, is Albert aware of this…?" The marquess lifted his head between Verity and James, a sneering curl prominent on his lips.

"I have a mind to drag you outside and cut your fucking tongue from your head," James murmured with lethal softness.

Verity flinched at the leashed violence throbbing in his tone, and James ruthlessly suppressed the need to pummel the marquess into the ground.

"James, please," she whispered so softly he almost did not hear her.

He peered down at her. Her eyes appeared so

wide and wounded, and the confidence he'd seen growing in her over the weeks was replaced by a fear that made him want to howl. She looked so vulnerable and soft. James would be damned if he let such an insult and dishonor pass any longer.

"Let's go," he said, ignoring the marquess as if he was refuse underneath his boot.

They walked away, and James said. "We are leaving." He could not explain the emotions gutting him.

Her slippers *clip-clopped* on the floor as she matched his pace. "Leave the ball?"

He stopped, and she halted and stared up at him, a worried frown splitting her brows. James glanced down the length of the hall, noting the marquess had disappeared. "Yes. I'll bring around my carriage, and you will plead a headache and make the necessary excuses to your mother or whomever you need to. If the marquess approaches you while I am outside, I do not give a damn about the scandal, you will kick him in the balls."

Her lips quivered, and a smothered laugh escaped. The tight tension around his heart eased. She'd laughed, the fear had been reduced. Part of his job had been done. The other...Lord Durham needed to understand the error he had made in touching Verity.

James smoothed a thumb along the curve of her lower lip. "Say it, Verity."

She cleared her throat delicately. "If that bounder should approach me, I will…I will deal with his manhood quite decisively. I vow it."

He felt a peculiar tightening in his chest at the vulnerability he spied in her eyes. James felt like a cad. Her soft delicacy would never have been enough to deal with a man like Durham on her own. And he had seen how badly she wanted that courage to stand up to her attacker if the man should ever approach her again. The pursuit he had just witnessed spoke of the odious character of the marquess, the surety he felt in his power and privilege.

He caressed her chin briefly. "I'll go bring around the carriage. Follow me discreetly."

She nodded, and he made his way toward the entrance but waited until he saw that she had slipped inside the ballroom safely. He collected his coat, and his carriage was summoned. James made his way outside, grateful there was no long queue to leave the ball, for it was still early. In fact, more carriages were still arriving.

He entered his coach, drew back the curtain and put out the lantern inside. James wanted a clear view of the outside without anyone knowing he was in the equipage. After several minutes and Verity had not shown, he decided to go back in. On that thought, he saw a young lady come outside. She glanced up and down the road, tugged her coat closer around her body to ward off the chill in the air, and then made her way to his carriage.

The coachman jumped down upon her arrival, knocked the steps down, and assisted her in. James felt relieved when she entered.

"In here is dreadfully dark," she gasped.

The coach rumbled away, and he leaned back against the squabs.

"Would you like me to relight the lantern?" The dark felt intimate, and wonderful, and provided him the opportunity to crave her without masking his expression of lust from her innocence.

"No, I do not mind."

"I am sorry for what you endured just now," he said gruffly.

"The fault is not yours."

Yes, it was. He had known of the marquess's dishonor for weeks now, and he had not rectified the matter. The only reason a gentle, refined lady as

Verity had done something so reckless as approach a stranger to learn how to fight, was because she had felt cornered and helpless with no defender to aid her.

"He frightened you just now. I am so damned sorry. I should call him out."

"Strike it from your thoughts." She sighed a bit wistfully. "I admit I was afraid when he first called to me in the hallway, but I assure you anger soon overshadowed my fear."

She said it defiantly, but even now there was a slight tremble in her voice. And at this moment, his Verity appeared more delicate than ever. Yet the set of her chin hinted at her stubborn streak and unique strength.

"I've always wished I could stare him in the eyes and let him know how much he truly hurt and frightened me. Let him know what a nasty blackguard he is. I wonder at the futility at wanting a confrontation like that. Even if he were to show surprising remorse, I would not forgive."

He gripped the edge of the carriage seat, fighting the need to draw her into his arms and merely hug her. That would be dangerous. The searing anxiety in her and the rage in him would reach for each other, and he would end up taking her virtue in a damn carriage.

"Sometimes to overcome fear, there is a place in us, a place filled with resilience and defiance that wishes to stand up to that fear. It will first start as a tremor, but then it becomes a roar that cannot be silenced. That is why you wish to tell him the pain he has caused."

A smile curved her lips, and he was enchanted, as an unexpected silence stretched between them.

"Where were you, James?" she asked curiously.

He released a rough sigh. "In Hampshire. I have an aunt and two cousins."

"An aunt and cousins? How marvelous!"

And then he told her everything, from the box to the journey and meeting his family.

"Oh, James you must be so delighted. I am looking forward to meeting your cousins. You will have to hire them the best of tutors and dance masters to help them take their proper places in society."

He grunted. "I'll most certainly need a wife to help with that. As it stands, my coarse manners might be more of a hindrance than a recommendation."

They fell into another deep silence, and he could feel her stare.

"Have you decided on a wife then?"

"Yes." And James realized he was unworthy of her. For he had been falling in love with her and had failed to make plans to protect her. How shortsighted he had been.

"May…may I ask the lady's identity?"

Was it his imagination there was a quiver in her voice and that it had hoarsened?

"No," he said softly, a tender hope stirring in his heart. Verity was affected by him.

She spluttered. "Well, why ever not?"

"When I have done everything I need to be worthy of her, I shall shout it to the world. I promise, you shall be the first to know."

She sniffed disdainfully. "If she does not know of your worthiness…she…she is a bacon-brained silly miss!"

Her voice cracked alarmingly.

"Are you crying, Verity?"

A few beats of silence, "Of course not, why would I be?" she then muttered, sounding as if she had been driven to the extreme limits of her patience. "I too have most excellent news. Viscount Stanhope has expressed an interest in courting me."

James's heart cracked, and the doubts worked deep.

"Is Stanhope a man of your choice or is he your brother's."

And James wondered if she wanted the man if he could respect her wishes and walk away. Denial clenched his gut into painful knots, and he breathed deeply. He never wanted to force her into any situation, not of her own choosing, not when so much had been taken from her. And if this Stanhope matched the kind of man she had always wanted.

Christ! James did not believe he could be honorable, it was more likely he would whisk her away until she consented to be his wife. James leaned forward and touched her trembling lip with a finger. "Answer me, Verity. Is he your choice?"

Her eyes sparked with wild defiance, and she haughtily tossed her head. "I've not made one as yet, and my brother will never be the one to decide whom I marry."

James sat back against the squabs, tumbling her answer over in his mind. Verity did not speak another word for the remainder of the journey. When they arrived at her home, he assisted her from the carriage. He walked her to the wrought iron gate and watched as she made her way up the steps and knocked on the door. It opened, she paused, and his heart jerked.

Turn around, he silently beseeched.

But after that slight hesitation, she swept inside, and the door firmly closed.

An irritable snort slipped from him, then James smiled. His Verity was furious he had selected his countess. And that was more than adequate to let him know their friendship was simply not sufficient for her, either.

CHAPTER 13

Vincent, my carriage will arrive for you by nine pm.

J.

Verity scowled at the succinct note, quite irritated with James. That sensation had been lingering in her heart from last night! Even worse, it had been the most restless night, for she was unable to sleep, tormented with the thought of James marrying Lady Anna or someone else. Surely their friendship would change. No wife would abide the close bond which they'd formed.

"I cannot lose you," she whispered softly, not understanding at all the wretched feelings inside her. With a sniff, she slowly opened the box, gingerly unfolding the clothes inside. Dark blue trousers with a matching tailcoat jacket, a gold waistcoat, white undershirt, and cravat. There was another box with black evening boots which were surprisingly her size and a dark brown wig.

She glanced at the note once more. James was taking her to the club. There was no other explanation. But why? And how had the dratted man thought she would be able to dress in these clothes? The doorknob to her room twisted and she narrowed her gaze. Verity had been very deliberate in her actions for the day, locking herself away into her room. Albert usually reached home from a ball or his club at dawn, fell into bed, and woke at noon. She had filled her breakfast tray and taken it into her room, all with the intention of avoiding him. The patience or perhaps strength to deal with him after last night's farce was just not present. Her family was blind to her pain, and she no longer wished for them to see and understand it. Verity desperately wanted to leave, be in her own home, and start a loving family not shadowed by betrayal.

Albert had pounded on her door at about one in the afternoon, and she had ignored all his threats and remained in her room eating the last of the breakfast scones when she got hungry.

"Verity?"

It was her mother. But she could not trust that Albert was not with her. Verity made her way to the door. "Yes, Mamma?"

"I would like to speak with you, my dear. Albert has told me of what transpired last evening at Lady Middleton's ball."

Verity made no reply, quietly waited with her forehead pressed to the door.

"Albert was very wrong in trying to manipulate you to make amends with Lord Durham," her mother said after a few moments.

Verity stiffened and stared at the door, almost wishing she could peer through it. She grasped the doorknob but did not open.

"Will you join me for tea?" Her mother asked.

It felt like an olive branch, and a lump formed in Verity's throat. "Perhaps another time, mamma. My head aches."

Her mother's sigh traveled through the hardwood door. "Will you attend Lady Escott's ball tonight? Lord Stanhope called earlier, and I was forced to inform him you were not well. Verity, I do not like speaking through this door!"

She glanced back at the box on the bed and everything it represented. A scandalous club and night of rousing impropriety. A night of freedom. "I hope you have a great time, mamma. I shall do a spot of reading and then retire early."

Verity moved away from the door, counting down the hours until her brother and mother departed for their evening of amusement. She sat before her small writing desk, opened the drawer, and withdrew a sheaf of papers. It had been a while since she had written to Aunt Imogen, at least two weeks.

> *Dear Aunt Imogen,*
>
> *The season progresses at an intolerably tedious pace. I find I am not overly enthused with making the social rounds with mamma and Albert. I miss the countryside. Inhaling the morning chill into my lungs, smelling the freshly mowed grass and your rose gardens. I dare admit that I even miss Vicar Pomeroy's outrageous sermons on the sins of fornication. I dearly miss our long walks through the countryside and to the village.* ~~Aunt, I have met a man: One lord James Radcliffe, the Earl of Maschelly. He is wonderful, and I believe I am falling irrevocably in love with him...~~

Verity crossed out that bit, a surge of fright filling her heart. In love? She bit into her lower lip, wondering if the way he made her feel was truly love? She continued writing to her aunt, chuckling at the irritation her aunt would feel at that crossed out bit in the letter. Aunt Imogen would still be able to read what Verity had intended, but the fact she had moved onto other topics would drive her aunt into a curious frenzy.

A few hours later, her mother and brother departed jointly in the carriage. Verity who had not gone down for the dinner gong, now rang the bell for her maid and requested a tray and a bath. Her stomach rumbled embarrassingly, and a few minutes later a tray arrived, and she quickly consumed the delicious, but slightly cold meal.

Next, she completed her bath, and as her lady's maid patted her shoulders dry with a soft towel, Verity said, "I will need your help in dressing quite wickedly for a masquerade ball, Lily."

The young maid's eyes widened then she bobbed with a quick smile. "Whatever you wish, lady Verity."

"I would like to be assured of your confidence. My brother and mother do not know I am to attend this masquerade and I will go and be back before they arrive. I rely on you to help me keep this secret, Lily!" she whispered conspiratorially.

Lily smiled. "I am right sure I'll not tell a soul. Not even my aunt. And I would never tell Lord Sutcliffe. None of us likes how he shouts at you, milady." She gasped. "Forgive the impertinence, my lady. I spoke out of turn."

Lily's aunt was the head cook, and the two were quite close. "Thank you, Lily," Verity said with a kind smile. "I shall not forget your kindness, and you have not spoken out of turn. And I too do not like how Albert speaks to me."

About fifteen minutes later, Verity's breasts were carefully bound with strips of linen. She then dressed in the clothes, wig, hat, and boots James had delivered.

"Lady Verity," Lily breathed. "You look quite the fancy gentleman. I wouldn't know it was you if I passed you in the streets!"

She laughed. "That is the aim, Lily. And I shall be off."

Verity added the cloak to conceal her appearance as she made her way down the stairs and through the back entrance. The coach waited near the mews, and she strolled over, confident she would not be recognized. Seeing her approach, the coachman hurriedly knocked down the steps, then gallantly assisted her into the equipage.

WHEN THE EARL WAS WICKED

A warm, clean, masculine fragrance filled the air. She closed her eyes and inhaled deeply.

"I wasn't sure you would be in here waiting. Are we going to the club? Or one of those wicked haunts of ill-repute it is rumored you've visited frequently in the night."

The figure seated opposite her shifted and piercing green eyes settled on her. "*What* have you heard about me and from whom?"

"Ladies talk?"

"Genteel ladies gossip of places of ill-repute? I am impressed."

She laughed lightly, aware of the increasing beats of her heart. "Why…why are we going?"

"There is a match I would like you to see."

How unusual. Before she could question him further, he asked, "Did you have nightmares last night?"

"No," she answered, turning her face away from his disquieting scrutiny. "My dreams were of a different sort altogether."

He stretched his long legs casually before him, and their boots touched. "Dare I ask?"

"An answer won't be forthcoming."

"Ah…those kinds of dreams."

This bit was drawled with such wickedness she

gasped and turned to him. The gleam in his gaze contained a sensuous flame, flustering Verity. The man looked at her enigmatically, and she sensed tonight would be different to all their other encounters.

The coach stopped, and he closed his eyes briefly. "Do you trust me, Verity."

"I do." Her answer was swift and uncompromising.

A spark of indefinable emotions lit in his extraordinary eyes.

"Have I ever told you, James, that you…your eyes are beautiful?"

A flash of teeth as he grinned. "Might I have a poem too?"

She choked on a laugh. "No. I am deplorable at that."

They exited the carriage and made their way to the club. She felt nervous, and she could not understand why. It was James. A coiled readiness seemed infused in every line of his body, and though his lips and eyes smiled, there was something hard and frightening behind the joviality. She sensed the bonhomie had been for her, to relax her perhaps.

They entered the club, walking down a familiar

long hallway to the interior of the gambling den. Raucous sounds of laughter, clinks of glasses, and snatches of conversations filled the air. They did not linger, wading through the excitement in the air, pushing past many lords and disguised ladies and made their way upstairs and to that fighting room.

Unaccountably, nerves jumped low in her belly with each step that took her closer to that large door. The bulky man guarding the entrance bowed, then let them in. It was the same as the first time she'd come, most of the room in shadows, but the ring in the center had several lanterns surrounding it. The deeper she went into the room, the more she could make out masked ladies and gentlemen seated before the tables, smoking cigars, and drinking liquor.

James took her to a table so perilously close to the ring she could reach out and touch the rope. Verity glanced around noting they were the only table so close.

"James?" she asked, hating that a quiver existed in her voice.

"All will be well, Verity, I will be back shortly. No one will disturb you here." His voice, though quiet, had an ominous quality.

What shook her the most was how silent the

room was. The last time there had been background chatter and a ripple of excitement. Now the stillness unnerved her.

A ripple went through the crowd, and she scanned the room then realized they all looked at a point behind her. She twisted in the chair and almost expired in shock. James was entering the ring bare-chested with his wrists wrapped, and on the opposite side another man, similarly clad, entered to face him, and it was Lord Durham. Verity experienced a gamut of perplexing emotions—alarm, relief, fear, and happiness. She stared at her shaking hands before breathing in roughly.

She mattered to James, for he stood, proud and powerful to defend her honor. Tears pooled in her eyes, and her heart ached as if it would shatter. Verity stood, and it felt surreal as she moved closer toward the ring.

The marquess danced lightly on his feet, keen anticipation in his eyes as he stared at James. But James stood there, his hands hung loosely at his side, his head canted left as he stared at the man. "I want everyone to understand this is not a match," James said, his voice traveling through the room. How cold and dispassionate he sounded.

"Of course it is," Durham said with a taunting

laugh. "The prize is twenty thousand pounds, and I've long wanted to fight you."

"That money will be donated to a women's relief society."

Durham's eyes glinted with mockery. "I see your sobriquet of the bare-knuckle king has led you to the delusion you will win this match. I plan to gamble and visit my favorite pleasure house." He licked his lips suggestively and some in the audience laughed.

"This fight is about justice, and a matter of honor."

She watched James with a terrible fascination, unable to take her eyes off his expression of ruthless purpose. His implacable mien was unnerving.

The marquess's face creased in a mask of concern. "What in God's name are you about, Maschelly?"

"You hurt someone I care about."

Everything inside of her went warm. Yet the silence around the two fighters was chilled.

The marquess's lips thinned. "I don't—"

James stepped closer and lowered his voice. Verity had to lean on the ropes to hear him. "This was years ago, and you have escaped the consequences of your actions. You attacked her, held her down, and tried to force yourself on her. You are a despoiler of innocence and beauty. You leave behind fears and nightmares. You abuse when you should protect. For that you deserve to die. There is no recognition in your eyes of whom I speak. And that tells me you have lost count of the faces you have hurt. You will learn a very painful lesson tonight, Durham."

Verity almost cast up her accounts. She had not been his only victim. Wild anger throbbed through her, it twisted and churned, until it became calm, and hinted of the darkness James had spoken about. This man had hurt her, possibly hurt other ladies or servants under his care because that was the type of man he was. Fury almost choked her.

Verity barely heard the announcer shout that the fight was about to start, that they followed the underground laws which meant no rules, and the purse was twenty thousand pounds. But she heard the final word as it was bellowed, "Fight!"

Both men moved toward the other with ruthless purpose. They both possessed similar raw-boned, powerfully built frames. Worry for James rushed through Verity, and she wanted to plead with him not to risk himself. The snake was not worth it. The Marquess danced in, his form graceful, and attacked. James shifted away with stunning agility and slammed a fist into the marquess's side. *Thwack.* Someone behind her gasped at the inherent power in that hit, and Verity's heart roared.

The marquess stumbled, and he shot James a dazed look, and she instinctively recognized that usually when contenders fought, it was not with such brutality.

You will learn a painful lesson tonight, Durham.

Verity pressed a hand over her mouth and watched in horrified fascination as James slammed another fist into the man's gut before he could recover. The marquess doubled over for a few seconds before he stumbled upright. Then James moved in and gave him no mercy.

Thwack. Thwack. Thwack. Thwack. Thwack. Thwack. Thwack. Thwack. Each hit echoed with the brutal and punishing force of their delivery.

And not once had the marquess landed a hit on James. The marquess tumbled to the floor, and she expected a cheer from the audience, but they remained quiet.

"Get up," James commanded.

It took him a few tries, but the marquess stood, swaying slightly. Verity winced to see the blood dripping from his lips, and the already ugly purple and black discoloration forming over his body.

Then James shifted to face her and held out his hand.

Her heart galloped and skipped a few beats, was he really holding out his hand to her and indicating for her to enter the ring? She breathed heavily, looking at his bloodied hands, unsure what James was thinking. But she trusted him unequivocally. She reached for him, and he helped her into the ring. She peered into the raw, brilliance of his gaze, uncaring they had an audience.

"You said, if one day you could tell him what he did…the nightmares would go away forever."

She inhaled in a shallow, quick gasp, then turned and faced the marquess. Verity felt helpless in the grip of sensations—rage, fear, doubt, daring—swelling through her body. She stepped closer and stared at the man who had caused her such pain.

"What the hell is this?" Durham snarled, swiping a bubble of blood from his lips.

The warm, protective heat of James's body moved closer. "She has something to say, and you will listen to every word."

"*She?*" The marquess peered at her from a

swollen eye, an ugly smirk on his face. "What did I do, not leave enough coins?"

She flashed him a look of pure disdain. "You took something from me: Peace and happiness, and you will not get another minute, you vile, revolting excuse of a man. You are a maggoty coward!"

Anger flashed in his eyes, and he stepped closer. Yet she did not feel intimidated. She stepped forward, felt James's start of surprise, but before he could stop her, she balled her fist and let it fly. Pain jerked along the bones of her arm, but with satisfaction, the marquess's head snapped back.

With a roar of fury, he charged at her, and with a nimbleness that rivaled James's earlier elegance, she danced from beneath his reach to behind of him. A murmuring of admiration swept through the crowd, but she did not direct her attention to their reaction. The marquess spun around, and Verity saw the perfect opening. She stepped in with sure swiftness and kicked him in the balls with all the pent-up pain she had lived with for almost five years.

An odd high pitch squeal tore from his throat as he tumbled to the floor, clutching at his man parts. Tears leaked from his eyes and sweat coated his body. No remorse filled her. Verity wished she could do it again when she thought about every other woman whom he might have hurt. All the other ladies who might not have had an aunt to rescue them. Or a brother and a father to defend their honor. Or a…James.

Verity stared at him, reached up and pulled the short wig from atop her head. It was important that he knew who had brought him to his knees. The marquess stared up at her, confused, and she still saw no recognition in his eyes. Unable to halt the need burning inside, she withdrew the pins that had ruthlessly confined her hair so and dropped them on the floor. The room had remained silent at this unusual display, and the clatter of hairpins seemed to echo loudly. Her hair tumbled over her shoulders in dark waves. The marquess gasped, and his eyes widened.

"You!" he spat like an oaf.

"Yes, *me*," she whispered, clenching her fist at her side.

The Marquess stumbled to his feet, his cheeks flushed red with rage and embarrassment. James came up behind her and rested a hand atop her shoulder. Comfort. Warmth. Safety. The touch had been brief, but it centered her against the tearing emotions ripping through her chest. Her lower lip trembled, and she felt the urge to cry.

"You will never look in her direction again," James said beside her with such lethal softness for a moment she felt afraid.

Then it vanished to be replaced with a warm glow of security.

"If you ever come close to her again, or even approach her, I will kill you," James murmured.

The marquess paled alarmingly. "Maschelly, I—"

"I will absolutely *kill* you." The cold, ruthless conviction settled in the space between them, and no one spoke or moved for several moments.

Then James turned and held out his hands. Without hesitation, she slid her hands in his, the thin leather strips preventing the soft, heated contact she wanted. Then he escorted her from the ring and to the side where he hurriedly put on his shirt, waistcoat, and jacket. He stuffed the cravat in his pocket, and they made their way through the stirring crowd who watched their departure.

When they neared the door, a lady in a green filigreed mask whispered, "Upon my word! Is that Lady Verity?"

A shadow seemed to detach itself from the wall

and stood in front of them. It was the owner of the club. "I do not need to know the offense, but I can tell it had been grievous, Maschelly," Viscount Worsley said, his gaze stark and compassionate. "Durham will be blackballed from my club."

James stared at the viscount. "He is a future duke."

Worsley smiled. "And you are my friend."

James nodded. The viscount's eyes touched on her face, and then he bowed. "Lady Verity."

It felt odd that her reputation had just been irrevocably ruined, yet here she stood, dispassionately unruffled. "Lord Worsley," she said, with a slight dip of her head.

Then she looked at James, and that was all that had been needed. Without another word, he led her through the smoky and raucous interior of the gambling den to his carriage outside.

CHAPTER 14

Once inside the carriage, Verity leaned back against the squabs, but a tight tension held her rigid. Her future was now vague and uncertain. All the plans of marriage and a future away from her family had been dealt a severe blow. But Lord Durham had been dueled using fists, and she believed the man would never dare to approach or look at her again. The certainty crawled into her heart, burrowed deep, and filled Verity with the most fantastic sense of peace.

I will absolutely kill you.

James's conviction had rung with ruthless truth, and she believed he meant every chilling word. As they stared at each other in the low lantern glow, her entire being seemed to be filled with a sense of waiting. She spied heart rendering tenderness in the gaze upon her body. Her heart jolted, and her pulse pounded.

"Are you hurt," he asked gruffly.

"There is a small ache in my arm, but it is not worrying. Thank you, James," she whispered.

"You should not be thanking me," he snarled, raking fingers through his hair. James's jaw tensed visibly. "Your reputation has received a severe blow. I will do all in my power to fix it, Verity."

"I shall not allow it. It was my choice to reveal myself to him in such a place. There is no need to take on any more of my burden."

"Nothing about you is a burden or could ever be. And you…you were a burning flame of fearlessness. Never doubt it for a minute."

His assurance wrapped around her like a warm blanket.

"Let me take you home, and tomorrow I shall visit—"

"No," she said with passionate certainty. "Take me to your home, James."

"Verity," he groaned. "The scandal of the season just happened. The news will be all over town like wildfire. The best place for you to be—"

Her heart leaped. "James."

They stared at each other in a tense silence that throbbed with perilous awareness. Nervously she moistened her lips. "I know what has been lost! My reputation…and the hopes I had for the season have vanished like ashes in the wind."

She held out her hands which trembled, and a smile quivered on her lips even as tears filled her eyes. "But I also know what I have gained: my freedom, my pride, and my honor. I am going to drink at least two glasses of whisky, and I shall not give a damn! Then I shall head home." A blush heated her cheeks at the profanity, and she glanced away from his unflinching regard.

James knocked on the roof twice and the coachman replied, "Yes, milord?"

"Head to my townhouse."

"Yes, milord." The carriage rumbled with speed as if the coachman had sensed the dreadful tension and urgency from inside. Once they reached his townhouse, he helped her down from the coach, and they walked up to the front door. He fished keys from his pockets and opened the door. The house was dark, and it was evident the butler had not waited up for him. They made their way to the library, where a little fire burned in the hearth, casting the room in more shadows than anything else.

He went to the sideboard and poured himself a drink. "Would you like a drink? The options are whisky, port, sherry." There was a dangerous edge to his tone.

She locked the door with a *snick*. A thick, heavy silence blanketed the library. Verity needed his kisses and soothing touch to calm the wild, primal urges throbbing through her. Steadying her erratic pulse was impossible. "When I first thought about approaching you for lessons, I was so nervous. Your reputation about town is one of such wickedness, James."

He glanced at her, before swallowing the contents of his glass in one gulp. The look in his eyes did something to her. The blatant heat and admiration caused her belly to tighten. "I've only ever seen the sweet gentleman."

His eyes lit with tender amusement. "Sweet?"

She sauntered over to him, lifted a finger, and stroked along his chiseled jawline. His hand darted out, snaked around her waist, and pulled her roughly, almost violently against his body. She inhaled sharply at the contact, tipped on to her toes, and kissed him, swallowing his grunt of surprise.

The empty glass dropped onto the thick carpet with a thud.

She kissed him, curling her tongue over his, tasting and consuming him, before pulling away to say, "Oh, yes, so *very* sweet."

The fingers around her waist tightened even more. "I want that wicked seducer that is whispered about," she breathed against his lips. "I never want to close my eyes again and remember another body atop mine. It must only be *you*."

"And in the morning?" he asked gruffly, gripping her chin, and staring into her face.

His touch was almost unbearable in its tenderness, and her heart knocked painfully inside her chest. "And in the morning…"

They stared at each other. He released her chin and thrust his fingers into her tangled hair. The hold was firm, domineering, and possessive.

"And in the morning, what will we be, Verity?" he whispered, his breath hot against her ear.

"And in the morning, we shall still be friends," she said hoarsely, tears pricking behind her eyelids. And Verity sensed it was a lie. Everything was different. Something had changed, but she couldn't identify what. And she could not imagine their path forward with the scandal that now surrounded her name.

Tears escaped and rolled down her cheeks. His thumb brushed away the evidence, and he stared at her with such desperate need she trembled. "Do you have any idea how much I've wanted you?" His uneven tone scraped against her senses with its rich sensuality.

"Then show me," she whispered achingly.

"Verity," James said, pressing a kiss of violent tenderness against her forehead. "I am *weak*...weak for you." The admission echoed like a curse. He brushed soft kisses on the tip of her nose, then her eyes, then briefly over her trembling lips. "I'll not be able to resist you, so for God's sake, please—"

She caught the rest of his words with her mouth and poured all the raw emotions pounding through her into the kiss. He responded, he took over, and he kissed her with ravishing expertise until she trembled in his embrace. His tongue slowly stroked hers, and she gave herself over to the hot, languid sensations building within her. She hadn't known... dear God, she hadn't known pleasure like this existed, not from a kiss. Verity became lost entirely in the taste, the scent, and the feel of him.

His large hands cupped her cheeks, their

mouths barely separated , and they breathed raggedly.

"This is adrenaline coursing through you. The hunger thrumming through you, the primal need always happens after a fight. It will pass, Verity." His tone was rough with an erotic warning as his hands tightened on her hips.

"What I feel for you, James will never pass. You torment my dreams. You enter a room, and my heart beats, and even long after I have left your presence, there is a smile, a happiness in my soul I cannot explain, only want to bask in. You make me feel, James. I feel bound by touch." She kissed the corner of his mouth, and down to his collarbone.

A harsh groan vibrated from his chest. Aroused shock almost felled her when he tugged at the buttons of her trousers and delved deep inside to her wet slit. She shifted, breathing deeply, certain she would collapse at his feet. Verity fisted his shirt and jerked to the tip of her toes when he pushed a finger inside of her. There was a tight pinch, a feeling of being stretched, and…and vibrant sensations of lust.

"I'll not fit," he said with such harsh sensuality a shiver tore through her.

She bit his lower lip and then sucked gently to

soothe the skin. Verity wasn't altogether sure to what he referred to, but she said, "You'll make it fit."

The unintentional provocative assurance settled over them like a heated, sensual blanket.

Holding her gaze, he slipped another finger inside of her, and a cry broke from her throat, a surge of heat arrowed through her belly and lower…to right where he had invaded. His fingers moved, a thumb raked over her sensitive nub, wetness coated his fingers, and a broken cry of need escaped Verity as she responded with wantonness.

He withdrew his touch from her wet sex, and holding her eyes with his, James undressed her. It took so much courage not to ask him to extinguish the lights. Everything felt so wicked. He removed the evening jacket, waistcoat, shirt, and cravat. He unwrapped her bound breasts with gentleness, but there was nothing tender in the gaze that stared at her breasts once they were revealed. He bent his dark head and brushed a light kiss over the mounds of her breasts. With a groan he lifted her into his arms with an arousing display of strength, walked with her over to the sofa by the windows, and lowered them, so she sat astride him.

"I want inside you." His voice was so deep, so rough now.

His hands roamed her naked body as if imprinting the shape and feel of her in his mind and heart. Her chest tightened with pleasure at the hunger on his face, and for the first time, Verity was confident he wanted her with a similar craving. Those diabolical fingers caressed over her nipples which were so hard they hurt. Down they went over her stomach and to her pulsing sex. He cupped her, the touch so possessive and domineering she felt a brief moment of uncertainty. James was a man of sensual expertise, and Verity was out of her depths.

His other hand stroke down the slope of her back. The touch soothed and reassured even as it seduced. "How sinful can I be, Verity?"

"Are there degrees of debauchery?"

"Yes." Lust flushed along his cheekbones and darkened his eyes. "I can kiss you here."

She stared at him blankly before his meaning came clear. Her entire body blushed, and it was so very hard to hold his stare.

His lips curved into an excitedly challenging smile. "I can protect your sensibilities or ruin them," he murmured, moving his diabolical fingers even deeper.

"Honesty," she gasped, holding his gaze. "I want your honest passion, everything you feel for me, and nothing less, James."

He pulled her forward, so she collapsed on his chest, dragged her up against his body, and kissed like a man who had been out in the cold for far too long and had finally found shelter. James twisted with her, and her back met the soft cushions of the sofa. Releasing her mouth from the bruising passion of his mouth, he placed a kiss in the hollow of her neck, then drifted over. The touch of his lips on her nipple sent a shock of desire through her body. But he did not linger, kissing over her quivering stomach to the top of her mound.

He knelt before her and lifted her splayed thighs on each side of his shoulders. Her entire body blushed red at the lascivious sprawl and the look of lustful greed on his face. Her fingers clenched in the cushions above her head as he dipped and stroked his tongue along the quivering softness of her abdomen. His lips disappeared, then the stroke of his tongue against her inner thigh, the rasp of his teeth as he nipped her flesh. Fire raced through her body.

The touch of his tongue as it glided over her nub was a caress of pure, nerve-wracking pleasure. His tongue caressed her sex, sensually teasing and passionately ravishing. Verity fought to keep from screaming with the intensity of sensations. Her body tensed, drawn tight as the pleasure built inside her. Verity felt as if she would shatter any moment from the overwhelming sensation of vulnerability and arousal washing through her.

She pushed up on her elbows and stared in dazed arousal at the dark head between her thighs doing wicked, filthy things with his lips and tongue that should have mortified her sensibilities. Instead, she felt free and wanton.

He alternately sucked on her nub of pleasure until she thought she would simply expire from the exquisite torment. "Oh, James, please!"

She had no notion of what she wanted, never imagined there could be such wickedness between a man and a woman. He flicked his tongue lower, devastating her with tortuous gentle licks. She wanted to scream, but she had the breath barely to whimper pleadingly. Verity knew later she would blush from the memory of how desperately she began to lift her hips to his devious mouth. She moaned helplessly with pleasure, her body sensitized, shivering, and trembling under the breath-taking assault of his erotic kiss against her core.

He stood and shrugged off his clothes and boots with alarming swiftness.

"Oh, James, you are so *bloody* beautiful!"

She gasped as he lowered his body over hers, lifted her legs to wrap them high around his back, almost up to his shoulder blades. Then he kissed her softly. "Nowhere near as beautiful as you, Verity."

He reached between their bodies, and a hard pressure nudged her entrance, then came a push. James stretched her, inexorably filling her. Verity whimpered at the painful feeling. He paused, sweat beading his brow and brushed a soothing kiss over her lips. Then he dipped even lower until he used his mouth to capture an achingly sensitive nipple. His tongue curled around her nipple, drawing a desperate moan from her throat as her hands gripped at his shoulders.

His hips flexed, and he buried himself deep in one powerful stroke. Verity cried out at the pain. Somehow his fingers found her nub of pleasure, and he rubbed, sending a striking pleasure through her body. Her wetness grew, her thighs trembled, and he pinched, pressed, and worked her nub until she screamed into the crook of his neck, waves of ecstasy tearing through her body.

"Oh God, James!" Her wetness was almost mortifying now.

But it seemed that was what he'd waited for. He leaned into her, holding her against his body as he began to pump inside her. James's groan was harsh, broken as he rocked her onto his hard length, riding her with a deep, driving rhythm. There was such pleasure, alarming pressure, and erotic pain at the tight fit despite her wetness, but she could not bear the notion of him stopping.

She clasped his sweat-slicked shoulders, her nails biting into his skin. Her cries filled the room as his thrusts increased. Ripples of pleasure peaked once more, and another release burst over Verity's senses, drowning her in unrelenting pleasure. He devastated her with his lovemaking and sensuality. For though she had peaked twice, James did not seem sated.

He rode her with such lust and passionate tenderness, Verity hugged him to her, and surrendered to the raw heat building between them. His arms tightened around her, and with a hoarse shout, he released into her, pulling another climax from her aching body. Her breath came in long, surrendering moans, and Verity collapsed weakly beneath him, shudders of her release still tearing through her.

He dipped and captured her lips in a deep passionate kiss, he suckled on her tongue, pulling gentle moans from her. She felt her core pulse around his member still inside her, and as if in reply it throbbed and hardened once more. He rolled with her so she sat astride him, not once releasing her lips, he savored her mouth. Then he started to move his hips upward into her sex. It was gentle at first, but then his movements grew hungry and relentless. Unknown feelings swelled inside her, urging her to use unladylike words to encourage him wickedly. Her sex grew hot and slick, and he continued, each stroke fanning the flame growing inside her belly. It felt glorious as his strokes vibrated through her body. She never knew such pleasures existed, never dreamed it possible.

The feelings crested and she exploded with a wild, wanton cry. His entire body jerked with power and he gripped her buttocks, holding her on his member as it erupted his seed deep inside her. They both collapsed breathing raggedly.

A few moments passed and they just stared in silence at each other. He then gently pulled from her and Verity had not the energy to move. She did not look up when he pressed a cloth between her legs, a handkcrchief perhaps, she was too busy blushing.

"Did I hurt you?" he asked gruffly.

"No," she whispered. "You were incredible." And the realization that she was ruined in every way settled on her shoulders.

He came down on the sofa and pulled her atop him. He pressed a gentle kiss against her forehead, and her heart climbed into her throat. It felt like a farewell. Panic and pain burst in her heart. It would have to be farewell on his part if he still had ambitions to marry a lady of quality. It was not only about himself now. But his aunt and cousins. Her ruined reputation would only serve to drag them in the gutter with her. And James knew it, and Verity could not avoid the knowledge. She buried her face into the crook of his neck, and they stayed like that for a very long time.

Blissful moments later, Verity's eyes fluttered open, and she realized she had fallen asleep. Panic rushed through her. Was it dawn? She shifted and smiled. James also slept. She gently disengaged from him, blushing at the ache between her legs. Dressing was a challenge, but she did it, grateful men clothes were so much easier to manipulate. Then, she walked softly over to the small clock on the mantle and held it to the dying fire.

It was almost two in the morning. Her mother and brother would still be occupied with their amusements. There was time for her to slip into her room before they arrived. Verity went back over to James and stared at his sleeping form.

I'll never forget you.

Then she turned and made her way outside to the waiting coach, befuddled as to why soft sobs were tearing from her.

CHAPTER 15

Lady V's fist of fury…or should we say kick of righteous anger? This author has not yet learned what dishonor a certain Marquess D dealt to a charming and evidently brave lady of the ton. Dressed in trousers and jacket, this avenging lady visited the notorious club in disguise and soundly defeated the marquess with a swift kick to somewhere unmentionable. It was as the marquess screamed his pain and embarrassment and fell to his knees, that his opponent was revealed to be a lady. I daresay a certain marquess will not recover from this public set down and humiliation any time soon—

With trembling hands, Verity lowered the scandal sheet onto the small end table in the drawing room. Everything inside of her urged her to go to James, even if it was only ten in the morning. Had he seen the scandal sheet? It was irrefutable proof she was ruined and would not be considered by the *ton* as a lady of quality anymore. She had known the risk when she had first approached him, and Verity would not dissolve into crying fits over the situation.

She closed her eyes, but it was a smile that came to her lips. There had been no nightmares last night. There had been no fear as her head hit the softness of her pillows. Only a weightless sleep. Just comfort. And peace. Even knowing her reputation was shattered into so many pieces, it could never be placed back together.

The hopes of marrying the man of her dreams were lost. She would have to travel abroad until the scandal died down. Even for a few years at least, though Verity was very aware society did not forgive or forget transgressions that stepped out of the bounds of decorum and civility. Perhaps she could travel to Italy or France, and once there she would meet a fair gentleman and fall in love.

A sob hitched in her throat. James occupied all the emotions in her heart and moving abroad to escape the scandal meant she would not see him for a long time. Perhaps when she returned to London after a number of years, he would have found himself a lady of quality and be married with children. The sudden pain that knocked against her chest strangled her breath. It was truly unbearable thinking of James with someone that was not *her*. It was agonizing thinking of living a life without him abroad, or even in England. It was James's kisses she hungered for, it was his arms she wanted to hold her whenever she was scared, and it was his eyes she wanted to peer into whenever they delighted with life.

Her hands fluttered to her lips. When…when had she fallen in love with him? For the wild and beautiful sensations swelling in her heart could be nothing other than the forever kind of love. But last night…last night he had said goodbye. She had felt it in his touch and the kiss he had pressed against her forehead.

Panic and a piercing loss rose in her throat. Did James feel any sentiments for her, or had she been the only one to unwittingly engage her heart? Had last night meant more to him than a wicked night of passion? It felt foolish to wonder, but she had a sudden burning need to go to him.

The door to the drawing room burst open, and her brother stormed in, his appearance one of great dishevelment. His hair was mussed, his cravat askew, his boots muddied. He was evidently only just returning from his night about town.

He waved a paper in the air. "Is it true, you silly, stupid girl?" he demanded, pinning her with an angry glare.

She paused to give him a polite, enquiring look. Her brother often spoke to her with a patronizing air which she found intolerable. Verity usually responded with cutting remarks and chilling hauteur which served to drive a deeper wedge between them. They were not as close as brothers and sisters ought to be, and with the ugliness of the past lingering between them, they never would be again. She stared at him with a contemplative air, quite pleased her pulse no longer jumped whenever he displayed such anger.

Her mother bustled in behind him, closing the door for privacy. She wore a green riding habit with a matching hat. The glow in her cheeks indicated she had just returned from her morning ride. "Verity?" her mother demanded, picking up the newspaper. "Albert believes this...this Lady V mentioned in the scandal sheet, is you? I have told him that it is absurd, but he raced ahead to confront you like a madman!"

"Everyone at White's believes it to be her. Why would they think that, mother? The very fact they think it is *her* is a catastrophe."

Verity poured a cup of tea with affected calm. "Lord Newsome's carriage ran off the road into an orange seller last week near the Smithfield market. He killed her, leaving the woman's four children orphans. They were sent to the poorhouse. Lord Newsome himself had been inebriated, and there were no consequences for him of course. It was all in the papers, and I daresay that is more of a catastrophe than anything else."

"Who cares about a damned orange ragtag beggar," her brother roared. He pulled the newssheet from her mother's hands and slapped it onto the table. "Do you know anything about this, Verity?"

She took a sip of the tea, closing her hands around the cup, needing the warmth that curled around her palms. "I cared," she said into the silence. "Another lord did too. He fought for them and set up a trust with the prize money for their future. Those children are now living in a proper home, their bellies are filled each day, and they are warm. There is enough money from that prizefight to ensure they live a very comfortable life and be afforded an education."

"For God's sake, Verity! You will answer the question or so help me I shall—"

"Yes, I kicked Lord Durham in his balls."

Her mother swooned, perhaps at the vulgarity of Verity knowing of a man's balls or perhaps the action itself. Albert caught Mamma and gently led her over to the chaise longue by the low burning fire. When he straightened and turned to Verity, his features were filled with wrath and a promise of retribution.

"How dare you speak so casually of your behavior and without any guilt," he lashed with raw fury.

Even though Verity did not feel as if she was obliged to offer any explanation, she said, "I am sorry my reputation has been portrayed in such an odious light for all of society to speculate on. But I cannot regret it, because I am at peace, Albert."

"Peace!" He threw her a fulminating glance. "How could you be so reckless, improper and indifferent to the disagreeable consequences of your willful ways! You have brought shame upon this family and have jeopardized our standing within society."

"No," she said with remarkable calm. "You did that by remaining friends with a blackguard who had attacked and hurt my mind, my body, my trust, and my pride. And I can only surmise now that you feel great shame that I, as a lady, had to defend my own honor."

He looked confounded by this forthright speech. "Defend your honor, Verity? Are you so foolish you have not seen that you have *ruined* your reputation? Who will have you now? I am just from Lord Aldridge's townhouse, and it took considerable convincing for him to agree that he will still have you despite the scandal. And that was after I persuaded him Lady V may refer to any other foolish hoyden! I am agog that you would sit here, proud of your actions, Verity. That incident with the marquess was almost five years ago, and you have held onto it with reproachable bitterness. You look at Mamma and me with unjust disappointment. What purpose would it have served for me to become enemies with the marquess over farfetched and unfounded accusations? He *denied* it most vehemently."

"I am your sister," she said, standing. "One whom loved you once, and I daresay you held affections for me as well. It was on that connection,

Albert you should have protected me. Instead, you acted in a similarly dastardly and cowardly fashion. It is I who am ashamed to call you, brother."

He stomped over to her, his hand raised in a threatening position to strike her. Verity shocked them both by smiling. Inside her heart pounded, her palms sweated, but she maintained an outward air of cultivated indifference. And Albert hesitated, apparently daunted by her lack of fear. "If you strike me, dear brother, I will not hesitate to retaliate in a similar fashion."

"My God, you've gone mad," he breathed.

She began to walk away, but he halted her, stretching to grasp her wrist. She wrenched herself free from his hold and went around him, anger rising in her chest.

"Albert!"

That sharp admonition came from their mother. She stood and stared at her children, and Verity was shocked to see the tears coursing down her mother's cheeks. They turned into harsh sobs, and Verity glanced away, her own throat burning with emotions.

"Mamma, I know this seems bad now, but I shall fix it," Albert murmured, going over to wrap his arms around her shoulders. "Her marriage to

WHEN THE EARL WAS WICKED

Lord Aldridge will render her respectable once more in society's eyes. It will take some time, but eventually, they will start inviting her to their drawing rooms and balls again."

"Oh, my dear boy," her mother said tearily. "We failed Verity in the most odious fashion. And it was our actions which forced her to act in such a wretched manner."

Her brother flinched, and she stared helplessly at her mother. Verity hadn't dreamed the countess would ever admit how they had wronged her.

"I am terribly sorry, Verity," her mother gasped. "I do hope you will forgive me."

"Mamma, your nerves are overwrought by this mess, you have nothing to apologize over," Albert retorted with a fierce frown.

"One day I will, Mamma, but it is not today," Verity said stiffly, and walked away, leaving them alone.

She ran up the stairs to her room, went over to her dressing table, and took up the sole pieces of jewelry she possessed—a sapphire necklace and earbobs. Gifts from her Papa on her fourteenth birthday, only a few months before he passed. She slipped them into the deep pockets of her day dress, shrugged on her pelisse and hat, and hurried back downstairs. Verity walked so fast it was almost a run. She did not want another confrontation with Albert before she could escape the confines of the townhouse. The butler opened the door for her, and she skidded to a halt.

James stood, his fist lifted to knock. He was dressed quite finely, and he had a bouquet of flowers—yellow and white roses—in his hands. He tugged off his top hat and slapped it against his thigh, the gesture an uncommonly nervous one.

"James!" she cried, startled. Then she said in a softer voice, "I was just coming to see you."

He was evidently discomposed by that admission. "Were you?"

"Yes."

He lifted an arrogant brow. "Am I to be invited in?"

She stepped closer to the threshold. "I would not recommend it. The atmosphere is poisonous."

A dark warning flashed in his eyes. "Are you hurt?"

"No, I am free." They stared at each other, and something warm and tender shifted in his eyes. He lifted the flowers to her, and she reached over the threshold and took them, dipping her face into their petals and inhaling deeply. "Thank you," she murmured, feeling a bewildering mix of hope and confusion.

"I have some poems too," he muttered.

It was then she noted a small brown book in his hand. During their lessons, he had sworn nothing could induce him to pen poetry and sonnets to a lady. Warmth burst in her chest like sunshine.

"But I confess they are terrible. I have been working on them since you left last night, without saying goodbye."

Verity flushed as the butler's eyes widened. James opened the small book and cleared his throat. "Your eyes are brown and golden, but they remind me of the brightness of a blue summer sky. Your lips are lush and thick, but in a most delightful rosy way and not like a leg of lamb. Your—"

Verity giggled, a horrified sound came from the butler, and at the same time her brother's voice rang out with a, "Good God, what is going on? Lord Maschelly?"

Verity looked over her shoulder at him, then stepped forward, grabbed James's arms and with a tinkling laugh ran down the steps, tugging him with her. He followed without question, and her brother bellowed in the distance. James assisted her into his carriage and sat opposite her.

"I am not going back into that house, *ever*," she said, conviction flowering through her soul.

He knocked on the ceiling, and the coach rumbled away. "You will not?"

"No. It has been unbearable for months, and I shall not bear it a minute more. I only have the clothes I am wearing and my dearest possessions in my pocket, but I do not care. My future husband is quite wealthy, and I daresay he will be able to replenish my wardrobe effortlessly. And when I come into my inheritance at five and twenty, we will be even better situated."

A dark shadow passed over his face. "Your husband?"

"Why yes, of course. I am three and twenty and do not need my brother's permission to marry the man I love, a man of my heart's choosing." Then she smiled at him. "May my Aunt Imogen live with us, James? I promise you shall love her."

He stilled, hope, relief, and something more profound darkening his eyes. "Live with *us*?"

Verity frowned. "Do you mean to say that atrocious poem was about *friendship*?"

He grinned, and her heart lifted. "No." He tugged at his neckcloth. "I love you," he then said simply. "I do not have the elegant words, Verity, or the flowery flattery, but I promise you, none will love, protect, and cherish you as I do. You fill every crevice of my being with happiness, and I cannot imagine a life without you."

She flung herself at him, and he caught her and gathered her in his arms. She rained laughing kisses over his nose, his jaw, and his lips. "I love you, James, so very much. I should not be saying this, because it does not bode well for me, but I am no longer a lady of quality. My reputation is damaged and may *never* be repaired."

He stared at her. "Verity, your qualities of strength and kindness are more valuable to me than a simpering miss with acceptable tonnish qualities. I love you, and since you have consented to be my wife, I'll not hear this nonsense about you not being…perfect. Marry me, Verity. Be my countess, my lover, and my friend."

She rested her forehead against his. "Yes, I absolutely will."

EPILOGUE

Two weeks later…
Birchmount Manor

Verity laughed breathlessly against James's mouth, her head spinning most deliciously from his ravishing kisses. He tasted of wine and his own uniquely arousing flavor. The thick verdant grass beneath her crinkled, and she slid her legs against his trousers, so very tempted to be naughty with him out in the open. They picnicked at the southern side of their estate, near the large and beautiful lake.

James lifted his mouth from hers. The gleam in his gaze contained a most sensuous flame and such burning love. "Have I lately mentioned how much I adore you, Lady Maschelly?"

Her heart jolted with delight. "Only about an hour ago," she whispered, fitting her lips perfectly to his for another deep kiss.

Desire curled in her veins, and she moaned softly. They broke apart, panting.

"I am still in awe that you are my wife, Verity," James said, pressing a kiss to her brow. "I love you."

She grinned. "I love you, my James."

He sat up, resting his back against the large beech tree they reposed under, tugging Verity into his arms.

"Another letter came from mamma today," she said, lacing their fingers together.

"She writes to you every day," James said. "How do you feel?"

"The pain lessens each day, but I am still not ready for more. I cannot explain my reticent; I only know it is there in my heart."

"Give it more time, my sweet."

They had married only two days after she had run away with him in his carriage. Verity had scandalously stayed in his townhouse until he procured the special license, knowing her mother or

Albert would not dare breathe a word that she was not at home.

Verity had written to inform her mother she was now the Countess Maschelly, and her mother had replied with good felicitations and a heartfelt plea to mend their rift. Her apology had felt sincere, and Verity recalled how her mother cried the morning she had left their townhouse. One day Verity would invite her mother to her new home, but the months and years of pain would not vanish because her mother wished it. Verity would continue to correspond with her through letters until she was comfortable with their relationship.

"So, this is what a love match looks like," a voice filled with amusement said.

Verity withdrew from her husband's embrace to face his cousin, Elanor, who stood staring at them with unabashed curiosity and laughter lurking in her dark blue eyes.

Verity laughed. "Yes," she said a bit smugly. "This is what it looks like."

"I daresay should I get married, it will only be for love," Elanor said wistfully. "Like what mamma had with papa… and what you both now have."

Then she smiled, dipped in a small curtsy, and

continued sauntering toward the walking path of the massive forest bordering their country estate.

"I hope she finds it," James said gruffly, staring after his cousin. "Our scandal might make their welcome in society difficult."

James wanted the best opportunities for them, and Verity echoed his sentiments wholeheartedly. To their delight Aunt Judith, Alice and Elanor had moved in with them at Birchmount Manor. At first, his aunt had worried that with the newlywed she would be underfoot, but Verity had reassured her that in a manor with over one hundred rooms, they each had ample space for privacy. Verity had also invited her Aunt Imogen to reside with them, which she had gladly accepted.

Verity rubbed his knuckles reassuringly. "Most of the mentions in the scandal sheets seem to admire my bravery."

"And they should."

"I think our hurried wedding is more scandalous than me kicking that odious man in his balls," she said with a light laugh, still amazed she could reference the marquess with no feeling of dread.

James's eyes lit with tender amusement. Verity was free of the marquess and her haunting memories, and she had her husband's belief and love in her to thank.

"And even with the scandal of our hasty marriage, society is insatiable for our presence at their balls and soirees. We've gotten so many invitations from our neighbors. We'll stay in the countryside for the next few months, and next year when we take Elanor with us to London, she will shine beautifully."

His hands tightened around Verity's waist, and she snuggled more against his chest. Verity felt such happiness she didn't know if she should weep or laugh.

"We should discuss babies," she murmured.

She felt the thump of his heart.

"What about them?"

"How many should we have?"

He seemed contemplative. "Seven."

She gasped, wiggled out of his embrace, and turned to face him. He had a grin on his face, and his green eyes glinted with deviltry. Verity laughed, snuggling back into the arms of the man who cherished her more than anything in his world.

THANK you for reading **When the Earl was Wicked**!

I hope you enjoyed the journey to happy ever after for Verity & James. REVIEWS ARE GOLD TO AUTHORS, for they are a very important part of reaching readers, and I do hope you will consider leaving an honest review on Amazon adding to my rainbow. It does not have to be lengthy, a simple sentence or two will do. Just know that I will appreciate your efforts sincerely.

If you were intrigued by Viscount Worsley, the lord who owns and runs the notorious gambling den, you can read his story, ***Sins of Viscount Worsley***, here:

Grab a Copy!

CONTINUE READING FOR A SNEAK PEEK INTO THE NEXT BOOK OF THE SERIES

A PRINCE OF MY OWN
Forever Yours Series Book 6

Excerpt

Grab a Copy Today

One tempting kiss may be her undoing...

Lady Miranda Cheswick is beautiful, witty, intelligent, and the family's great expectations are for her to marry a prince or a duke! A duty she intends to fulfill despite the craving in her heart to marry for love. An accident leaves her stranded at the country estate of the enigmatic and charming Dr. Astor, a man to whom she is inexplicably attracted.

Dr. Simon Astor has little expectation of making a grand society match. His sole focus should be on caring for his patients and raising funds for the hospital he hopes to build. However, the delectable and witty Miranda tempts him at every turn, he soon finds himself falling for her irresistible charm, and wants to marry her. Except Miranda's mother's devious plot will test Miranda and Simon's resolve. Is their love strong enough to triumph?

CHAPTER ONE

Lady Miranda Elizabeth Cheswick's first memories were of her mother extolling her great beauty, and that she would one day marry a prince, or most certainly a duke. As the daughter of one of the most renowned and influential earls in the realm, it was expected any match she made was to a man of rank, respectability, and great fortune. To that end, her mother, the Countess of Langford, had made it her duty since Miranda's come out three years ago to hunt a gentleman who fit those standards of the Cheswick family, with a single-minded intensity that Miranda admitted could be frightening and at times embarrassing.

Of course, her mamma did not regard her

matrimonial fervor in the same light. The countess had often said Miranda's incomparable beauty, grace, charm, and wit could not be wasted on a gentleman of mediocrity, and over the years the countess had impressed upon her daughter that very belief. And for so long Miranda had faithfully believed her beauty should only allow for the best in her life, and that belief had cost her the dearest of friendships. A friendship which Miranda had treasured. The rift between her and Pippa, the new Duchess of Carlyle, was so terrible they had not spoken in almost two months. And there was nothing Miranda wanted more than to mend that relationship.

She slowly lowered the newssheet which mentioned the Duke and Duchess of Carlyle were back in town after several weeks of traveling. A visit must be paid at once, and despite the fearful ache in her heart and the doubt rising inside, there must be no delay.

The door to the drawing room swung open then slammed shut as her mother marched inside in a swirling green dress and swishing petticoat. Miranda had been waiting for over two hours for this confrontation, for nothing had gone how her mother had planned it last night. She braced for the severe scolding that was about to be delivered.

"You will not disappoint our expectations ever again, young lady," her mamma cried without any preamble, her violet eyes brimming with tears and unjust reproach. "It is your duty to this family to marry and marry well! I'll not hear any more objections, Miranda!"

Miranda sat on the chaise longue, her spine rigid yet elegantly poised, daring not to blink as her mother scolded her most ferociously for yet another failure in snagging the man everyone had said was the catch of the season. "Mamma, I can explain—"

"Three eminently suitable suitors you have lost now! *Three.* You encouraged the Grand Prince Vladimir Konstantinovich to turn his regard to Miss Harriet Shelby, and now they are engaged! Why I still cannot credit it, a Russian prince with that nobody! Then the Duke of Carlyle was ripe for your plucking. I did everything to ensure you ensnared him and somehow, you foolish girl, you allowed him to get away. And I had the Marquess of Blythe conveniently locked in the conservatory with you at last night's soirée! I had to pay a servant to discreetly deliver a note to you and the marquess, and you…you had the nerve to slip through a window to escape!"

Papa had often remarked fondly of the devious ways mamma had secured his hand for marriage more than twenty-five years past. It seemed her mother required her to act similarly and did not hide that it was her expectations. She lifted her chin, hating to recall the shock of horror she'd felt last night when she realized what her mother had planned. "Mamma, Lord Blythe inspires little emotion in my heart."

Though the marquess was declared as handsome and a man of fashion and elegance, whenever he touched her, she felt cold and unmoved. Miranda had begun to wonder if passion truly existed. "He has never asked me about what I like to do or how I spend my day. He only compliments my beauty and—"

The countess shook her head as if in a daze. "You ungrateful, wretched girl! We have worked so hard to cultivate your reputation as a diamond of the *ton*, and you speak as if you wish it were not so!"

Over the last few years, Miranda had become a well sought-after social butterfly, coveted by the young bucks of each season. During the social season, her days were spent assisting her mother in ordering the household, planning balls, musicales, routs, and picnics. She was admired often by both ladies and gents for her exquisite grace and form when dancing, and her skill at the pianoforte. It was often remarked that she would make a fine wife with her excellent upbringing, amiable disposition, and breathtaking beauty.

"An engagement should have been in the papers today!"

Her mother's cries were like a stone scraping against glass.

"Mamma," she said, standing, her heart pounding with discomfort for she had never been one to contradict her mother. But the situation had becoming intolerable, the season no longer fun and intriguing. Until recent events, Miranda anticipated each season with elation for all the thrilling events she would attend and the courtship dances. She had been enthralled by the excitement of attending lavish balls, picnics, carriage rides, and walking out and flirting with several suitors. Now, only dread knotted her stomach whenever she thought about the next season and the marriage mart. "If I am such a sorry disappointment it is little wonder you do not banish me from your sight to the country with grandmamma."

That would be far more tolerable than the constant pressure from her mamma to secure any eligible gentleman that came on the market. The tedium of country life was vastly more appealing than the parties of the little season. In Lincolnshire, she could take long walks, visit the orphanage her grandmamma sponsored, and perhaps attend a few balls at the local assembly. But most importantly, there she would have space and the freedom to think about what she wanted from life, and not what her mother insisted she must possess.

"This season you have put my nerves out of sort most abominably, and you danced with Mr. Brandon last night! Why would you do something so foolish?"

With a sigh, she pushed a few loose wisps of hair behind her ears. "He is very good-natured and charming mamma, and he is the younger brother of a viscount, so he is not without connections." And he had appeared so earnest and anxious when he asked, she'd not the heart to reject him, and she'd had a wonderful time dancing the quadrille and the polka with Mr. Brandon.

The countess advanced further into the drawing room, the glint in her eyes a dangerous thing to behold. "You will politely decline his offer if he should approach you again. He is not the sort of man a young lady of your connections and propriety should extend the smallest encouragement even if it is only dancing!"

Her whole life it had been impressed upon her the type of man she was to marry. A prince. A duke. Her mother would possibly accept a marquess if he possessed considerable estates and wealth. There had never been a mention of the man's character, and it saddened her to realize it honestly did not matter to her mother or to most society members. Invariably she shared a similar truth. The men who pursued her had no liking for her mind nor were they curious about learning about her. Her beauty, connections, and dowry were all that was admired.

Her mother sniffed as if holding back tears. "The entire day I've despaired with your father about what we should do with you. Miranda, you are two and twenty. You should be running and organizing your own household. Why, at eighteen I was already with child with your brother."

"Mamma please, might we enjoy the rest of our stay in town without conversations about whom I'm to secure?"

Her mother stiffened as if she could not indeed countenance such a suggestion. "We planned to receive an offer this season! By next week everyone will be off to their country estates, and all opportunities will be lost until next year. Despite all my efforts in securing you a proper match you have willfully thwarted my best efforts."

Her mother's best efforts referred to the Duke of Carlyle, a man who had gone on to marry Miranda's friend, Pippa, in a rare and beautiful love match of the season a few months ago. Her mother's wicked wiles and Miranda's foolish heart had allowed her to go along with her mother's disastrous plan to compromise the Duke of Carlyle. Mamma had been determined for him to be her son-in-law, and Miranda had been committed to becoming a duchess. She had snuck into the man's room at a house party a few months ago, with the sole intention of compromising his honor so he would be forced to marry her.

The very memory of that scene had humiliation and shame crawling through her veins. She felt as if she aged several years since. Once she had taken it as her due that a man would look upon her face and fall hopelessly in love. That with a smile she would be able to ensnare him. She had rested much upon her beauty and had ignored her honor and common sense to her undying shame. "I do not wish to attend Lady Peregrine's house party, Mamma. Might I travel down to grandmother instead?"

Her mother's eyes narrowed. "That is our last event before we retire to the country with your father. I have it on good authority Lord Blythe will be in attendance, and I expect, young lady, an offer from him by the end of the party."

"And am I to secure that offer by any means?" she demanded scathingly with pain and anger beating in her heart. "Did you know I was silly and willful enough to try to compromise the Duke of Carlyle a few months ago, doing exactly as you suggested, Mamma? I slipped into his room at Lady Burrell's garden party! And Mamma…I went only in my banyan."

Shock glazed her mother's eyes, and she moved forward with jerky steps. "And he did not offer for you? How outrageous and dishonorable of him!"

Miranda rubbed her temples, hoping to soothe the headache she could feel forming. "Mamma, it was *my* conduct which was outrageous. He should have thrown me out on my head! Instead, he did the gentlemanly thing by walking away. And I was so humiliated at my failure I did not tell my dear friend the truth, and she then waged a campaign to destroy the duke's reputation when it had been unwarranted. Since then my eyes have been opened, the shame in my heart laid bare, and the regret in my heart heavy."

Her mother stared at her for several seconds. "You are simply too harsh with yourself, my dear. It was my expectation that you would secure the duke this season. It is a disappointment we must all bear, and it does us no credit to speak about what happened at that garden party. We shall rally and prepare for next season the best we can. I do have high hopes regarding Lord Blythe. While not the title we had hoped for you, the marquess has considerable estate and wealth. Now hurry to your rooms and ensure all is well for our journey in the morning."

A girl of your astonishing beauty must only marry a prince…or a duke…, I declare to be so! Refrains she had heard from when she was a twelve year-old child in the schoolroom. Words which had made her once preen, her chest puffed with pride, now made her feel sick to her stomach, and her throat aching with unshed tears. "If you'll excuse me, Mamma."

She left the drawing room and her mother, but instead of heading upstairs, she collected her pelisse and bonnet having already called for the carriage.

Almost thirty minutes later, she made her way to the townhouse of the Duke and Duchess of Carlyle in Portman Square.

Miranda bravely knocked on the large oak door, and when the butler made his appearance, she asked to see the duke and duchess. He allowed her inside and led her to the drawing room where a merry fire crackled in the hearth. She tried to marshal her thoughts, unsure of what she would say to Pippa and to the duke. The words eluded her, and the only guidance she had was the awful ache of regret in her heart and the burn of tears lodged in her throat.

"Miranda!"

She whirled around at her name to see a glowing Pippa gliding into the room. Shock tore through Miranda when Pippa enfolded her into a warm hug. There was no help for it, a sob tore from her throat. "Oh, Pippa, I have been so wretched with shame at my conduct. I have used you ill, and I am so very sorry!"

"Hush now," Pippa said, her own voice choked with emotions. "I regret leaving on my travels without mending our fences. You had apologized to me, and I ignored your overtures. Come, let's sit and talk." Looping their arms together, the duchess led her over to the sofa closest to the fire. The warmth seeped into Miranda's bones, thawing the cold knot of doubt which had constricted her muscles.

A sound alerted, and she glanced up to see the duke. Miranda flushed, discomfort crawling through her veins. She had slipped into this man's room and had shrugged off her robe! The room had been very dark, and she had doubted he even knew it was her, but the very memory of it made her want to die of humiliation. She stood. "Your Grace, I am so very sorry."

He smiled warmly, rendering her mute. "That is in the past, Lady Miranda. If I recall, more than five months ago. I probably should not say it, but without your antics, my darling Pippa would not have turned her mischievous wiles in my direction, and I would possibly have missed my love. So, I should be thanking you, hmmm?"

A laugh hiccupped from her. "You are both very generous, and I thank you for it."

And there was an easing inside that swelled and expanded through every crevice of her being. The duke lingered for a few minutes, engaging her in discourse before he excused himself. Miranda turned to Pippa, "You do appear radiant, Pippa. I am so pleased with your happiness."

Her friend squeezed her hand. "I cannot wait for you to find similar happiness. With your great beauty and poise, any day now—"

She tugged her hand away from Pippa. "Do you also believe a man would only be interested in me because of my beauty?" she cried. "Oh, Pippa, I do not want that! I want the gentleman whom I marry to see beyond that and see me! I want this even as I wonder who I am, Pippa. But I am most certain, I want to love the man I marry and also to know beyond doubt that he loves me just as ardently. I want to share my fears and dreams, and failures as they come and know I will always find comfort in his arms. Is it silly of me to hunger for this?"

Pippa smiled gently. "Oh, Miranda, it is an inescapable fact that you are lovely. You enter a room and men stare covetously, ladies glower in envy, many mothers worry you will outshine their daughters. Each season you receive numerous offers which your mother rejects. It is inevitable a man will see your beauty first, but I daresay if he is worth his salt, he will hunger to know the passionate heart that beats within you. And if he is fortunate for you to return his regard, he will then discover how kind and caring you are. How filled with good fun and humor, how passionate you are about art and music and I daresay he will love you."

She hugged her friend tightly. "Thank you, Pippa, I needed to hear this."

"I missed you," Pippa said softly, returning her fierce embrace. "I miss our long walks and talks. Let's promise nothing should ever come between us again."

"I promise it," Miranda said.

Almost an hour later she made her way home, a new purpose growing in unchecked leaps and bounds in her heart. From the age of twelve, she had been relentlessly groomed on how to become a wife, how to organize and run a household, and how to select charitable organizations to sponsor. Most attachments she'd observed throughout the seasons appeared cold and impersonal, with both ladies and their lords seeking other lovers to soothe the heartache of loneliness. She couldn't endure such a union. The notion of marrying a gentleman for his monetary worth and title, without possessing an ounce of regard for the man no longer sat well with her.

Miranda hungered to find her own place within the world which did not solely follow her mamma's guidance. She did want a prince of her own, a gentleman who would love her as she would love him, a gentleman with whom she could build a happy life and home. But for the first time since Miranda's come out four years ago, she secretly pledged to only marry a man she loved and one who possessed similar sentiments.

The Marquess of Blythe was the next man her mother had deemed a perfect match for her daughter. Such was his consequences that he could pick any of the debutantes of the season and they would fall gratefully at his feet. It was generally thought his age of five and fifty could be overlooked for his vast fortune and immeasurable connection. Indeed, her mother expected her to overlook the matter, and completely ignore that she would want to marry for a more tender sentiment.

This time she was determined to be the one to choose the man she wished to walk with, to dance with at balls, and to admire. *Don't worry, Mamma, I will ensure he is a prince…or a duke!* And that way she would not disappoint her family's expectation of her, but she would also be true to her heart.

WANT TO KNOW WHAT HAPPENS NEXT?
CONTINUE READING…

FREE OFFER

SIGN UP TO MY NEWSLETTER TO CLAIM YOUR FREE BOOK!

To claim your FREE copy of Wicked Deeds on a Winter Night, a delightful and sensual romp to indulge in your reading addiction, please click here.

Once you've signed up, you'll be among the first to hear about my new releases, read excerpts you won't find anywhere else, and patriciate in subscriber's only giveaways and contest. I send out on dits once a month and on super special occasion I might send twice, and please know you can unsubscribe whenever we no longer zing.

Happy reading!
Stacy Reid

ACKNOWLEDGMENTS

I thank God every day for my family, friends, and writing. A special thank you to my husband. I love you so hard! You encourage me to dream and are always steadfast in your incredible support. You read all my drafts, offer such fantastic insight and encouragement. Thank you for designing my fabulous cover! Thank you for reminding me I am a warrior when I wanted to give up on so many things.

Thank you, Giselle Marks for being so wonderful and supportive always. You are a great critique partner and friend.

Readers, thank you for giving me a chance and reading my book! I hope you enjoyed and would consider leaving a review. Thank you!

ABOUT STACY

USA Today Bestselling author Stacy Reid writes sensual Historical and Paranormal Romances and is the published author of over twenty books. Her debut novella The Duke's Shotgun Wedding was a 2015 HOLT Award of Merit recipient in the Romance Novella category, and her bestselling Wedded by Scandal series is recommended as Top picks at Night Owl Reviews, Fresh Fiction Reviews, and The Romance Reviews.

Stacy lives a lot in the worlds she creates and actively speaks to her characters (aloud). She has a warrior way "Never give up on dreams!" When she's not writing, Stacy spends a copious amount of time binge-watching series like The Walking Dead, Altered Carbon, Rise of the Phoenixes, Ten Miles of Peach Blosson, and playing video games with her love. She also has a weakness for ice cream and will have it as her main course.

Stacy is represented by Jill Marsal at Marsal Lyon Literary Agency.

She is always happy to hear from readers and would love to connect with you via my Website, Facebook, and Twitter. To be the first to hear about her new releases, get cover reveals, and excerpts you won't find anywhere else, sign up for her newsletter, or join her over at Historical Hellions, her fan group!

Printed in Great Britain
by Amazon